Tacones (high heels)

Tacones
(high heels)

Todd Klinck

Anvil Press

Copyright © 1997 by Todd Klinck

All rights reserved. No part of this book may be reproduced by any means without the prior written permission of the publisher, with the exception of brief passages in reviews. Any request for photocopying or other reprographic copying of any part of this book must be directed in writing to the Canadian Reprography Collective (CANCOPY), 6 Adelaide Street East, Suite 900, Toronto, Ontario, Canada, M5C 1H6.

This book is a work of fiction. Resemblances to people alive or dead is purely coincidental.

Printed and bound in Canada by Kromar Printing
First Edition
Cover design: JT Osborne
Cover photo: Angela Lee McIntyre

The Publisher gratefully acknowledges the assistance of the Cultural Services Branch of British Columbia, Ministry of Small Business, Tourism and Culture.

Canadian Cataloguing in Publication Data

Klinck, Todd.
Tacones (high heels)
Fiction.
ISBN 1-895636-14-0
I. Title
PS8571.L58T32 1997   C813'.54   C97-910200-6
PR9199.3.K485Y32 1997

Represented in Canada by the Literary Press Group
Distributed by General Distribution Services

Anvil Press
Suite 204A—175 East Broadway,
Vancouver, BC
Canada   V5T 1W2

dedicated to
Joan Klinck and John Palmer

INSPIRATION: Troy, Felipe baby, Mary (aka Chloe, Sylvia, Amy, Nicki, Sandi, etc...), Suje, Haven, Rod, 'Lil Bro' Jason, Andrew, Michelle, Skitchy, Snatch, Bev Ridge, lsd, Mistress Sheeva, the Real Girl, Abigail, Andrea Allejandra, Rosio Pantoja, Carolina, ChiChi Rodriguez, Lilandra Leon, Paola Devine, Charo & Nicole Batista, Mr. Villa, la Co Co, Luis, "Mother", Chad Connors, Annie Sprinkle, Chi Chi la Rue, coke, Brujeria, Wu Tang Clan, Tricky, cannabis, Diamanda Galas, "750", "5", the Om, "656", "270", the Studio, Sneakers and the original Tacones.

ACKNOWLEDGING: my family, my friends, all at Anvil (especially Brian & Heidi), Barricade Books Inc., Julie Berman, Bruce LaBruce, Canadian Male, Alan Causey, Jaffe Cohen, Tracy Dawson, Bob Desjardins, "el Convento Rico 2", Tony Fong, Victoria Glencross, Sujinder Juneja, Larry Kardesh, Michael Klinck, Donald Martin, Jason McLean, Mario Parada, Robert Robinet, Jay Siddall, and David Zurak.

Quotes with reference to Biastophilia / Gerontophilia taken from the book *The Encyclopedia of Unusual Sex Practices* by Brenda Love. Copyright 1992 by Brenda Love. Used with permission of the publisher.

SPECIAL THANKS: Judith Rudakoff for guiding, supporting assisting & encouraging.

AUTHOR PHOTO: Tony Fong.

AUTHOR'S AGENT: John Palmer, 32 Monteith Street, Toronto, Ontario, M4Y 1K7 (416) 967-7455.

The author can receive correspondence online at "spridle@interlog.com". You can visit the Tacones webpage @ http://www.interlog.com/~spridle/tacones.html

Table of Contents

1./Nobia Gets Pepper Spray in Her Eyes	9
2./Tacones: Headquarters	12
3./Blaine, Carrie, and the "Ex-Baby"	18
4./Trevor's First Ad	23
5./The Beach	26
6./The Trip Out Room	28
7./Elastic Throat/Strap Ons	32
8./Very Hot Baby and the Clumpy Maxi-Pad	36
9./Mr. Bell	40
10./Public Service Announcement	44
11./Trevor Places the Ad	47
12./A Date for Diva	49
13./Biff & the Boys	51
14./Peony	54
15./Nobia & Biff	57
16./Answering the Phone	59
17./Mr. Hammer	61
18./An Ikea Moment	64
19./Oops!	67
20./Emaciated	70
21./Isabel	71
22./Piss Interests & Heroin	74
23./The Fight	78
24./The Perfect Fuck	81
25./Ashley Sinks	83
26./Bungee Jumping	85
27./BIASTO-GERONTO-PHILIA!	89
28./Soozi	92
29./Full Service	96
30./Scrap	99
31./Surreal Drug Art of René Suvuomo	101
32./The Donut Shop	107
33./Ashley Bobs	109
34./Trick with No Dick	110
35./Ashley Rises	117
36./Crowd Thins Out	118
37./The Car	122
38./Isabel Weeps	124
39./Speed	126

1.
Nobia Gets Pepper Spray in Her Eyes

Nobia is pronounced No-VEE-yah. Because in Spanish the b and the v sound are kind of interchangeable, depending on which country you're from. Nobia is a beautiful transvestite. And hooker. And fighter. She goes to gay bars dressed in cut-off shorts that are slit up the side all the way, with pantyhose and very, very, high spike heels. She sits in the bars, sipping her drink. She never stands. She finds the highest stool to sit on top of—like she's overseeing everything. Sometimes she performs. Beautiful Spanish ballads. Once, she was disqualified from a drag competition because they thought she was too open about being a hooker. She fought them and they let her in and she got second place. Her roommate is another Spanish transvestite hooker. Maria. They live with Nobia's boyfriend Biff, who just got out of jail, and Maria's high school girlfriend Kate. The girlfriend is blonde and beautiful and very young. She is going to high school in the suburbs and is the valedictorian and Prom Queen. She thinks she's very open-minded and cool compared to her friends. And she is—the fact her boyfriend's a transvestite hooker being a good indication.

Another guy hangs out there too. Pedro. He's young, pretty innocent, hangs out with all the drag queens. Sometimes he dances for them in their shows. A lot of the time him and Kate hang out at Maria and Nobia's apartment while the two girls are out hooking. They watch TV and talk about high school, because Pedro's in high school too. He hangs out with gangs when he's in his Scarborough 'hood and drag queens when he's downtown. He knows the whole hip-hop lingo and attitude and is the class clown. Everyone from Scarborough thinks he's totally straight. Several gangs really think highly of him. As in, if he wanted to get someone killed, he could get it done in a second. But if they found out that he sometimes danced backup for drag queens in gay bars wearing just a sequined G-string, they would kill him. Literally.

11:30 p.m. Friday, August 30.
Little Italy, Toronto.

Kate is sitting in the apartment watching TV. Biff is out with his friends. Maria is in the bedroom snorting cocaine. Kate knows about this, but doesn't partake. She doesn't mind though. They all hear a loud noise. It's Nobia opening the door hard enough that it hits the wall. She comes in, looking like shit. Her eyes are red and puffy. Her mascara is all over her face. Her hair looks pretty rough. She is carrying one of her six-inch heels. The other is nowhere to be seen. She is barefoot. She is calm, though.

Maria comes out of the bedroom, wiping cocaine off her nose. "What happened, darling," she sniffs.

"Some trick spray me with pepper spray in the eyes," she says calmly, going straight to the bathroom.

"Oh my god . . . my darling . . . " coos Maria. "Are you all right?"

"I am fine. I did not see for one hour. I go to hospital. For a couple hours. But my heel still hit him in the forehead."

Nobia is known for her heels and she is known for her self-defense techniques. She dresses like a woman, but when she's hooking on the stroll, she fights like a man. It wouldn't be too unlikely to imagine that she's killed someone. But that kind of stuff isn't talked about.

Kate: "What's it like getting pepper spray in your eyes?"

"Hurts very painful. Where's Pedro?"

"Canada's Wonderland. He'll be back later. He's sleeping over."

Nobia has washed her face and reapplied her makeup and fixed her hair. She goes into her closet and gets out another pair of high heels. Pink. She looks flawless, once again. She goes into the bedroom and snorts the line of coke off the dresser that Maria had been cutting when Nobia came in. Maria leans down and cuts another one for herself and snorts it.

"OK. I go back to work," says Nobia.

No one really says anything. This is typical Nobia.

2.
Tacones: Headquarters

At Tacones, the after-hours club. This club is below a donut shop on Yonge Street, kept open by a combination of a strong security team and strong police force bribery. "Tacones" means high heels in Spanish and sometimes if the patrons are particularly fortunate, the Spanish drag queens show up at about 4:30 in the morning, out of their minds on booze and coke, and perform a show. And the shows are breathtaking. They are really wild, these Spanish queens. They do the most dramatic songs and wear elaborate costumes and have big choreographed numbers, with back-up dancers and special effects.

2:30 A.M. Saturday, August 31.
Tacones, Yonge Street, Toronto.

Stephanie is talking to Trevor. "This guy got a parasite . . . or some infection thing from fucking a cat. Can you imagine?"

"Fuck."

"And it wasn't the first time the medical community had come across this."

"Fuck . . . I don't know why people don't wear condoms when they fuck animals—it seems so obvious!"

Stephanie laughs because she thinks this is a really bizarre thing to say. Trevor doesn't. It really is obvious to him that people should wear condoms when they fuck animals. He is really into cleanliness, which outweighs the idea that one's desire for animal genitals might be wrong. Besides, he probably doesn't think it's that wrong to fuck animals. As long as it doesn't hurt them too much.

ACROSS THE ROOM . . .

Carrie and Blaine click their beer cans together in a toast "Cheers, baby," they say to each other. "Freedom at last!" says Carrie. "I'll drink to that!" says Blaine. He pulls out a cigar—the most expensive one he could buy at the all-night supermarket—and lights it. Passes it to Carrie. She takes a puff. "I think we're going to finally get along, eh?" she says. "Yeah, baby, we are," he says. They are both numbingly high on crack, having just taken a hit a couple minutes prior to this.

The host and owner of Tacones, René Suvuomo, is an eccentric, wild man who constantly looks like he is on the brink of running. He always has a cordless microphone in his hands, which is broadcast into all of the rooms in Tacones, even the VIP lounge. He is a big, big cocaine dealer. He has been deported from the States twice, which is why he is in Toronto running an after-hours club. He owns four houses and seven cars in Dallas. His family lives there, living on savings from his past crimes, and who knows what else. His mother works at the club, bussing the tables, doing dishes. She gets up on a chair behind the bar and watches the drag shows. "I like the mans when they dress like girls and singing," she says in her broken English.

René greets people when they come in the door, announcing their arrival to everyone on the microphone. "*Ay . . . Papito y José . . . muy bonito, muy bonito . . .* " followed by the cackle—his cackle more famous than anything about him. Someone once said "I used to live down on College on the fifth floor of a walkup and at five in the morning I'd wake up hearing that cackle and think—Yep, René Suvuomo is coming home . . . ." The laugh is undoubtedly annoying as hell but no matter how many times one has heard it, they can't help but laugh, too. René Suvuomo has a huge jerry-curled do, gelled shiny; a pointy goatee, tinted glasses, always wears loud cowboy boots (like red or pink or neon green) and crazily assembled ensembles of overalls, bellbottoms, knickers, bullfighter outfits, priest gowns . . . In the winter he wears an ankle-length long-haired fur coat. It has a really high collar and is possibly the most flamboyant coat in existence.

He goes into his office every ten minutes or so to snort coke with someone, or by himself. He is very hardcore with this.

Like never longer than ten minutes between snortings. Then he runs around everywhere and talks to everyone and cackles (in the microphone). He believes in his club, he believes in people who want to party all the time, who want to be high all the time. He doesn't have much need or respect for people who aren't like this. He doesn't have sex—he hasn't had much sex in the twenty-seven years he's lived in Canada. He has lost literally hundreds of his friends to AIDS and he says the only reason he doesn't have it is that he declined their daily invites to go to the parks or the baths or just about anywhere nasty where men shove their unprotected cocks into each other.

Diva is the bartender. He always works barechested, showing off his perfectly muscled upper body. Sometimes he just wears a jock strap. He is the image of a muscular jock straight guy, at the right angle. Until he opens his mouth. Then it's all over. He is very, very bitchy. Very effeminate. He is not the All-American Boy next door, even though he can pull it off.

Sample, Troy comes up to order at the same time as Jerry.
JERRY: Canadian.
Diva stares at Jerry, in disbelief.
DIVA: You think I'm serving you?
JERRY: Canadian, please.
DIVA: *(shaking head)* Uh uh . . . No way.
JERRY: What the fuck'd I do to you?
DIVA: You were fucking rude to me . . . that's what.
JERRY: I wasn't rude to you.

DIVA: You blew pot smoke in my face.

JERRY: When?

DIVA: Last night over at Daddy's Place.

JERRY: It was a total accident. You walked right in front of me.

DIVA: But it went in my face. And everyone in this city knows that I HATE pot. *(to* TROY, *who has been waiting)* What can I get you baby?

TROY: A coke, please.

DIVA: A coke.

TROY: Yes, please.

DIVA: Just a coke.

TROY: Yes, please.

DIVA: Yeah whatever, all right. A coke.

He opens it up.

JERRY: Can I have a Canadian?

DIVA *ignores Jerry.*

DIVA: Two dollars baby.

JERRY: Excuse me?

DIVA: *(snapping)* Just a minute! *(to* TROY*)* Two dollars honey . . . can you find it?

TROY: *(handing him a five)* Thank you.

DIVA *puts three bucks on the bar.* TROY *pushes the money across the bar as a tip and starts to walk away.*

DIVA: Hey!

TROY: What?

DIVA *hands him back a two-dollar coin.*

DIVA: Honey that's a bit of an excessive tip on a coke, you know? Take this.

TROY: *(in disbelief)* What?

DIVA: Three dollars on a coke, you know, what are you trying to do? *(to* JERRY*)* So are you sorry that you were rude to me motherfucker?

JERRY: No, not really, man. I wasn't fucking rude to you.

DIVA: *(snarling)* You piece of shit you were fucking rude to me and that's that. Now be gone! Out of my face!

DIVA *waves the guy away with his hands as if shooing away an insect.*

TROY *takes the two dollars and looks stunned.* JERRY *punches the bar, pissed off, and walks away.* DIVA *puts the dollar left on the bar in his tip jar, goes into the little kitchen off to the side and does a bit of coke from his long baby fingernail.*

3.
Blaine, Carrie, & the "Ex-Baby"

5:45 P.M. Friday, August 30.
Parkdale high-rise.

The baby is crying. Carrie and Blaine are sitting in the living room.

"I hate it. I fucking hate it. I know I shouldn't say that about my child, but fuck Blaine, I have to be honest sometimes even if it seems evil. I fucking hate the baby and resent it and think I made a wrong choice by having it by not aborting it and I feel those feelings towards it every single day and I feel guilty but I can't get the feelings away from me 'cause they're HONEST and they keep surfacing."

Carrie is crying. She is a mess. Blaine is sitting across the room in an armchair, staring straight ahead. Not saying anything.

Carrie continues. "I don't want it anymore . . . what do I do? Can I give it up for adoption now, or am I stuck with it?

My mother won't raise it. Blaine . . . I don't like fighting with you all the time . . . we never fought at all before she came into the picture." Carrie says all of this quickly, hysterically, jittery, on the edge of losing control. Tense.

Little Ashley continues to cry in the playpen in the kitchen. Her diaper hasn't been changed since the day before and her ass is getting progressively more itchy. She has only eaten Fruit Loops for the past three days, because Carrie threw a box into her playpen, but her rations are almost gone. Carrie and Blaine don't know that Ashley has started to develop scurvy. If they had taken her to the doctor, it would have taken about twenty-five tests to figure out what Ashley was suffering from. The doctors would have marveled at that fact, noting that the last time people had scurvy was when Canada was being settled and the settlers had no access to vitamin C. But now vitamin C is in EVERYTHING, they would think, and wonder, and question . . . . It's even in cheese.

Blaine continues to stare ahead. But he isn't oblivious. He has been thinking about the issue at hand as well. He has been trying to make decisions. He speaks.

"Do you support me in the idea of killing her?"

"Are you serious?" Carrie is freaked out. She is so romantically excited that he read her mind.

"Yes."

Carrie squeals with delight and happiness like someone who has just reclaimed something lost, and runs across to him and jumps on his lap and kisses him and hugs him.

"You're amazing, you know? You are."

Blaine just sits there, cuddling his girl. He feels very warm as well. He loves her. He has hated the year and a half of fighting over the kid. The kid who ruined their lives.

"Let's do it then."

"Oh . . . how should we?"

"Pillow. It's the quietest and least messy."

"OK." Carrie gulps a bit, because she knows she should feel some guilt. But she isn't feeling guilt. This troubles her, but an overwhelming excitement quickly rushes in. The excitement of something new, a change in a life that has gotten stagnant.

Blaine gets up, picking up a pillow from the pull-out couch that Carrie was lying on. Goes into the kitchen. Carrie follows along. She doesn't want to just be the "girl", hiding in the living room while her boyfriend kills her baby, she wants to support him, and maybe hold half the pillow. She wants it to go smoothly, to symbolize the start of something new and beautiful with her man. Blaine approaches the crib. Ashley shuts up, sensing that something is wrong. Blaine pushes the pillow over her face, causing her to fall back. He holds the pillow tight, muffling her screams. Carrie holds down Ashley's flailing legs. She stops her thrashing and screaming and Blaine keeps pressing the pillow into her face. He pushes as hard as he can. His face is pitch red and sweating from the strain, all his muscles are flexed, his legs are spread and braced. (He is not wearing a shirt and Carrie notices at this moment how much growth the steroid cycle he started last week has induced in his muscles.) He is pressing so hard that you would imagine her little skull to be squished. Finally, what seems like minutes later, he releases the pillow. Ashley is motionless. Her face is kind of blue. She is dead. (Definitely deceased. Bleeding demised. Passed on. No more. Ceased to be. Expired and gone to meet its maker. Late. Stiff, bereft of life, resting in peace. Pushing up the daisies. Rung down the curtain and joined the choir invisible . . . she is an **ex-baby.**)

Carrie turns to Blaine and hugs him.

CARRIE: I love you so much. Thank you. Thank you.

BLAINE: I love you too, babe.

CARRIE: What are we going to do now?

BLAINE: We'll drive to my Grandpa's house in the Bluffs . . . take his little dinghy out on the lake . . . put her in a garbage bag . . . tie a couple bags of sand to her 'cause Grandpa has sandbags at his dock, and toss her into the deep water.

CARRIE: Grandpa will let you use the boat?

BLAINE: Ah . . . if he doesn't we'll just take it . . . it's happened before . . . they know what to expect from me.

CARRIE: Mayhem. Right?

BLAINE: . . . and disorder. Mayhem and disorder. Back to normal, eh, babe?

This feels so amazing to them—a sudden click back to the connection they had before the baby—two intelligent people who liked to spend time with each other. Blaine grabs a garbage bag and they put Ashley in it and put the garbage bag into a duffel bag.

("If anyone asks, I can say we're having a picnic and the food is in the duffel bag," offers Carrie. "Good idea," says Blaine.) He heats up the crack pipe. "We have one rock left, babe," he says. "We should do it before we get into the car, and stop by at Mickey's on the way to Grandpa's for some more."

"All right," she says.

He passes the pipe to her. She smokes. He smokes.

They are both exhilarated now. Glad that they have never left each other. Glad to have each other. They hold each other for a couple of minutes.

4.
Trevor's First Ad

Friday, February 8, 1996.
Toronto.

Writing an ad for his escort service for the first time. Wonders if he should say "Big cock" or "Big, fat, juicy piece of man meat." Decides to use his real name. He feels like being slutty, but also feels like slutty sex would make him puke. The whole (not-for-money) gay world slutty sex scene stresses him out. Ulcers. He wants to emphasize that he is a service person, that he wants to please the client. It's the only way he can think—it's how he's always been: working at the bookstore, the law office, waitering, bartending—he's always wanted to please the customer. Except this time, for once, he will be benefiting personally from pleasing them. He won't be pleasing them and giving the profits to a corporation. If they want him to piss on them, they'll get it. Steaming. He wants to treat them like humans, even if they aren't. He thinks they'll come back if they like him. He thinks that he can do the best for himself and the world if he's not working as part of the system. He doesn't know how he feels.

FIRST TIME ESCORT — want to make appointments with serious clients who want to try out my services. I'm creative, intelligent, eclectic, and real. I've got a nice big 8-inch uncut cock, I'm 20 years old—I've got boyish looks and a muscular body (although I'm not a massive body-building type). I've got a pierced nipple and navel and a shaved head. I'm available for unrushed 1-hour sessions at my place downtown. Call me and we can discuss what you're into and make some kind of appointment. If my call forwarding is on, connect to me and ask for Trevor. If my call forwarding is off, and you can leave a number, do so and I'll get back to you. Discretion is assured.

Trevor tries recording the above a couple of times on the phone system. They have a section for escorts. He is nervous and uncomfortable and wants his voice to sound a certain way. He decides to rewrite it.

I'm a first-timer—I'm creative, intelligent, eclectic and real—and I want to make appointments with serious clients who want to try out my services. I know you don't only care about my mind, so I'll tell you about my looks which won't disappoint you. I'm 20, boyish-looking, with a shaved head, pierced nipple and navel, a muscular build—I'm not a body builder but I think my body is

*hot. Trust me that communication is the key to hot sex
and because I have a brain on my shoulders this will
help you to get what you want—give me a call or leave
a message if you can be reached.*

Too wordy. He thinks it is too wordy. He always gets too wordy. He can't just say something in a phrase or two. He is too much of a perfectionist to let it be said without details. But this time he thinks his ad should be pretty brief. Let them call and find out more if they want. But he isn't ready for the ad yet. Hangs up the phone. He has to wait a bit.

5.
The Beach

6 P.M. Saturday, August 31.
The Beaches.

Little girl on the beach by the boardwalk with her parents and baby sister. She is about three or four, this girl, and she is wearing a floral print dress. She is trying to climb a chain attached to a wooden jungle gym. She successfully makes it to the top, about seven feet in the air, and jumps down to the sand. She jumps up and down in glee, proud of her accomplishment.

A little boy is on the beach, playing in the sand, zipping up and down the beach, picking up flat stones, trying to skip them on the water, doing cartwheels, causing general mayhem. He passes a tampon applicator, and stops briefly, picks it up, blows on it like a whistle, throws it back in the water, continues running around.

Two grubby kids are playing with their mother. She looks

pretty tired, their mother, and they keep falling in the sand, getting the once-white T-shirts and shorts ensembles browner and browner. They both have ice cream all over their faces.

The rich girl sits under an umbrella on her *Beauty and the Beast* towel, reading her book. Her mother lies in the sun next to her, bronzing her thick-as-leather skin some more.

Diva is standing by the water, letting the waves almost hit his feet, but not quite, staring at three sand castles in the process of being eroded by the waves. Each wave hits them a bit more, causing a few million more grains of sand to fall back into the water. The little sticks that the kids put into the castle, probably to represent a flag pole or something, fall. The waves lap the castles away. Diva watches. He hasn't gone to bed yet. He's been walking around in thought since about noon, when the club closed. He feels pretty good.

6.
The Trip Out Room

René Suvuomo has a flair for drama. In the daytime he gets together with actors and others and makes them read for him into his video camera. He has them convinced that he is a video artist, and that he is working on an "artistic" project and that's why he can't afford to pay them. If necessary, he convinces them that he'll make them Hollywood superstars one day—that always works with the shopping mall food court clerks. They don't know that he is just using them for his own enjoyment, and to make quality videos for the Trip Out Room at Tacones.

It was said that René Suvuomo does not have any use for people who do not party but there is one exception. René Suvuomo has use for these sober people if they can provide something for him without the erraticness of junkies. René Suvuomo knows tons of cokeheads and alcoholics who can do electrical wiring for him, who can fix the beer fridges at five in the morning, who just seem to be . . . around . . . all the time with many skills. But there are some things René Suvuomo has to use the outside world for. And the actors are one of these things. He needs them to be dependable and work during the day when René Suvuomo wants to work. Most of the junkies sleep during the day. René Suvuomo does not. He never stops working. He doesn't sit around watching TV. He almost doesn't sleep. He is always up to something. That is the one main difference between him and all of his friends and acquaintances. That is also why he is lonely.

René Suvuomo does not like hallucinogens, but because he wanted to build the best club possible, he built a Trip Out Room, complete with surreal videos and two low, leather couches. Because René Suvuomo uses cocaine and believes he understands everything that there is to understand in this world, he believes that he himself is qualified enough to create the Trip Out videos. He knows that he can be weird enough, and subversive enough, and creative enough to create amazing videos for hallucinogen-heads. And he is. (As it will turn out later, several years after his final imprisonment, he really is an incredible artist. His tapes will be compiled and made into a two-part movie series. *The Surreal Drug Art of René Suvuomo, Volume 1 and Volume 2*. The videos will sell all over the world, develop a cult following and receive mention in the *New York Times, Time, Variety, Entertainment Weekly*, and other big American press.)

2:50 A.M. Saturday, August 31.
Tacones.

Tonight in the Trip Out Room, two little club kids are lounging on the couch, watching the TV. It's at the "Manline" sequence that René Suvuomo created. He phoned up Manline, the personal ad company, and transcribed, word for word, choice ads. He then got people he knew, actors, friends, to dress up in the appropriate look and read the ad into the video camera, as if it were their own ad.

"Hello! Um, I'm attractive, I'm considered cute, I'm box 9332—Um, I've heard others who expressed an interest in bondage and I'm quite sure that that's fun and stuff but, to be quite frank, and I'll get to the point . . . I'm interested in wearing diapers, and I'm wondering if other guys are into the same. Um, and if they're not into it maybe they've expressed an interest or desire. Um, I'm quite open just to talk or to um, maybe just meet. This is sort of new to me and maybe we could get together and explore this fantasy. I'm very discreet and very caring and considerate, so . . . and I'm a normal guy. So *(laughs)* let's talk, OK? I'm sure you know who you are. There's not a hell of a lot of us, um . . . who enjoy the same. But if you do . . ."

Bae and Breezy, the two club kids laugh hysterically. Not making fun of the ad but laughing at how funny it sounds to them.

In their Ecstasy World. They think it is beautiful that someone would place an ad like this. Bae actually is thinking of phoning it himself. Just to talk to the guy. He thinks it'd be interesting to meet someone brave enough to admit that he likes wearing diapers.

7.
Elastic Throat/Strap Ons

2:55 A.M. Saturday, August 31.
Tacones.

Blaine and Carrie's high is getting good. They've been doing crack zaps in the back room, drinking a fair amount of beer, and have smoked a couple of joints. (Carrie also took some Halcion. And a couple of Percocets.) The Lake Ontario baby deposit went smoothly and they've been chilling out at Tacones for a while. They are talking and holding hands and being genuinely cute. Carrie's reminiscing about their meeting . . . "'Member when we met?"

BLAINE: Yeah.
CARRIE: At that Colombian after-hours in the west end, right?
BLAINE: Yeah.
CARRIE: I was working as a stripper then.
BLAINE: Yeah. Me too.

CARRIE: Yeah. We talked shop.
BLAINE: Not for long, though.
Carrie laughs.
CARRIE: Yeah, we ended up in bed pretty fucking quick, didn't we?

Blaine laughs. "Sexy pussy," he says.

"Fucking huge tool," she says back, grabbing at it through his pants. "I want to suck it. Right now."

"Go for it," Blaine says.

"All right," she says. She goes down on him, pushing him against the wall, taking his drink out of his hand and putting it on the floor with hers. A few people sort of turn and watch, and many don't pay attention. She sucks Blaine's cock up and down, swallowing it all the way. Carrie has a very elastic throat when she's in the mood. Blaine moans in total pleasure.

"I'm getting right off on this being right here out in the open darling," Blaine says into her ear when she comes up for a kiss. She just smiles back and goes back down on his rod.

Eventually she pulls up her skirt and goes to put his cock in when he stops her—"Got a condom?" and she looks at him and laughs and nods and says "Yeah . . . we shouldn't make the same mistake twice now, should we," and he laughs too as she takes out a condom and puts it on and mounts his cock and rides until they both cum, noisy orgasms.

This sort of sexual behaviour almost never happens at Tacones, which is probably why tonight no one tries to stop them. No one knows how to react, because though they are pretty sure it isn't really the thing to do, no one is quite sure what is and isn't ordinary behaviour anymore.

CARRIE: I love it. You're back now.

BLAINE: Yeah. I feel good about this.

Her cellphone rings. She answers it.

"Hello? Which ad are you calling about? What would you like to know? I'm 5 foot 8 inches, 125 pounds, blonde, big breasted, firm stomach and ass, and a shaved pussy with labia piercing. Yes, I can get into strap-ons if you want. It's $200 for that service. Um . . . OK . . . (*in dirty voice*) You'd better fucking call me in twenty-five minutes so that I can bend you over and fuck you hard like the dog you are. (*normal voice*) OK? Call me in twenty-five, I should be home. You won't be disappointed."

"Fuck."

"Client?"

"Yeah."

"Which ad?"

"Dominatrix. He's a kinky one too. He made me demonstrate that I could be verbally abusive."

"Well, I guess you satisfied him if he's coming to see you."

"Yeah. I'm not really in the mood. But I guess I should try to do one."

"Yeah. I'll go with you."

"No, you don't have to. You can stay here if you want. Hang out with your friends."

"No, I don't mind. I'll take you home and then go wait in the donut shop."

"Get us some more, OK? For after."

"OK."

Blaine goes off to get. He buys extra, smokes the extra out in the back, with a buddy of his. He doesn't want to tell Carrie. He goes back up. "'K, ready to go?"

CARRIE: Yeah. Let's go.

They get in a cab, take it back to their place. Carrie goes upstairs. Blaine goes to the donut shop.

8.
Very Hot Baby and the Clumpy Maxi-Pad

6 A.M. Friday, August 30.
Scarborough.

Mother wakes up at 6 A.M. The alarm sounds nasty to her. She doesn't want to deal with it at all. The three kids are still sleeping. The baby at the foot of her bed, and the twins in their room. She gets up and looks in the crib. "There's my baby . . ." she coos.

She goes to the bathroom. She is in the second day of her period. That is always the heaviest flow day for her. She doesn't feel too great. Crampy. She always feels dirty when she's on her rag. She can't get clean no matter how long her shower is. She looks at her maxi pad when she takes it off and almost pukes. It is especially clumpy today. On days like this, she wishes menopause would have already come and gone.

She flushes the toilet.

It wakes up the twins. She hears them go off like rockets.

Bouncing up and down on their beds screaming before they even have their pees. They are extremely hyper and she doesn't really like that. They are also both boys, so she doesn't know how to relate to them. But they are good kids.

She gets in the shower and washes herself. In between her legs she scrubs and scrubs and scrubs, the water turning pink. She even takes a loofah brush to her genitals. It feels good on her clit, but she feels nauseous and dirty, so she can't even enjoy the sensations. The kids are now waiting at the door for her to finish, so she rinses off, puts on her robe, and opens the door.

"Good morning," she says. "Good morning mommy," they both say.

She goes to her room and gets dressed. Picks up the baby, dresses her and brings her downstairs to the high chair. Sets her in it. The baby drools.

The twins, upstairs alone in the bathroom pick through the garbage can. Pull out the used Maxi pad. "Open it up!" urges Patrick. Julian opens it up and they look at the clumps of blood. Fascinated. "Sniff it!" urges Patrick. Julian sniffs it. "Taste it!" urges Patrick. Julian tastes it.

The boys come downstairs, dressed. Patrick's hair is sticking up. "Comb your hair," she says to him, puffing on a cigarette. She just started smoking in the morning. She never used to smoke in front of the kids.

The boys eat the food she's put on the table. Cereal, an apple, a pop tart, 2% milk. They are all ready. She picks up the baby, the boys carry her purse, they lock the door for her, they all get into the car. Patrick and Julian fight and frolic in the back. They get along with each other almost always, mother notices. They only fight in fun, and they never leave each other's side. It's almost romantic. She periodically watches them in the rearview mirror. They are sitting in the very back part of the station wagon, where the seat faces a different direction than the others. They like to sit back there, riding backwards, playing games. She drops them off at the car pool drop-off point and goes to work.

In the office, she sees all the other ladies. Drooping hair, bad makeup. Mother feels so much better than the rest of them. But understands why they let their hair droop. Most of them have kids as well. Lunch time takes a while to roll around, and she decides to go to a restaurant with her co-worker Carol.

Carol is a wild party woman. Mother swears Carol is still on some kind of drug, because Carol is talking breathlessly and acting all forgetful. They get in the car. "Man, last night was crazy, man . . . I went out dancing at this club, got all fucked up on Jack Daniels, took some acid, danced for hours . . . I got laid too." Mother smiles and laughs. She isn't totally innocent, but is starting to not relate to the girl's free spirit anymore. She's not much older than her, either. They get to the restaurant. Seated, Carol asks "How's your baby?" Mother says "Ashley's fine. She's well behaved. The boys have a lot of energy, but other than that, they're pretty good kids. But she just sleeps and smiles and eats. Never cries."

Carol goes, in her hippy supportive way: "I think kids are right on, man. You created something from your body. They are a part of you. I think that's beautiful. Even if your life seems hard now, kids are great and you're great for having them."

They pay the bill and go back out to the car. The sun has broken through the clouds. Mother gets in. Carol gets in the other side. The car is stifling. The vinyl seats are on fire, almost melting. Mother turns on the air conditioner right away, then reaches into the back seat to get her sunglasses, which she left next to the baby seat. She sees the baby's little legs and starts screaming and freaking out. Carol looks to see what she's screaming about and sees the baby, still in her seat, face totally red, body limp and breathless. Mother goes into shock. She forgot to drop the baby off at day care. Baby is now dead.

9.
Mr. Bell

1 A.M. Saturday, August 31.
Toronto.

Donald Bell is walking along Maitland Street. Wearing little white shorts, a white T-shirt, sandals. Carrying a purse.

He sees Louis and Angel crashed out on the sidewalk in front of the convenience store. No cardboard underneath them, no blankets, no pillows. They're not asleep, just chilling out.

"Oooohhhh Kids! You shouldn't have to sleep on the cement. No one should have to sleep on the cement. You can come sleep at my place tonight."

The groggy kids are not so groggy that they forget their street senses. They are a bit hesitant, and figure that this guy's going to want something.

"You can have a good long sleep, and use my laundry and showers after. I won't disturb you. And listen, I'm not trying to get you guys for sex . . ."

"Do you think you could possibly give us a bit of money?" Louis asks. "We haven't eaten for two days."

"Yes. That's right . . . you need money . . . I'll give you each $100, all right? That way you don't have to get tempted to steal my things in the night, 'cause if I hadn't offered yous money I'd a deserved to get my shit ripped off."

Louis whispers to his girlfriend Angel, "Let's go."

"He probably just wants a blowjob or something," she whispers back, getting up.

"Money first," Louis says.

"I don't have it on me—upstairs. Don't worry kids, I'm not a sickie!"

They follow Donald Bell to his high-rise condo with 24-hour concierge. Up to the penthouse level. Donald Bell has a 3-storey penthouse. The men are waiting. Two of them grab the kids and inject their arms. Kids get stoned really fast. They feel numb. Very awake, but very numb and complacent. Very obedient. Angel is fourteen. Louis is thirteen.

"You got some, eh?" asks the camera man.

"I always get them, honey," says Donald Bell. "Now bring 'em to the bedroom!"

The security men grab the kids and carry them to the bedroom. Start to strip their clothes off—but Donald: "No! I want to make 'em undress each other. I want some tension!"

The clothes are left on. The camera man sets up the lighting equipment. Gets the camera ready. "'K, rolling," he says.

DONALD: OK Kids I want you to pretend we're not here,

and you're gonna make love for us. You are lovers, aren't you?

LOUIS: Yeah . . .

DONALD: Let's see some kissing, let's see the tongue. OK Louis, kiss her on her neck, lower, lower. Lift her shirt and lick all over her stomach, lick in her bellybutton. Lift her shirt higher, over her head. Lick around her breasts. Don't take the bra off yet. Just lick around the edges, dart your tongue under the fabric toward the nipple. OK Angel, I want you to moan like you're really excited by all this attention. Moan, ecstasy! Yes! And now grab at his cock through his jeans like you just can't wait to get to it. Like it's candy. Like it's the most important thing in the world. Unbutton his jeans. Stick your hands down the front. Stroke his cock. Unbutton the jeans more. Let us see your hand inside his underwear. Pull his cock out. Take his shirt off. OK Louis, take her bra off and lick her nipples. Lick them, suck them, pay attention to them. Angel, I want you to lick his cock around the head, up and down the sides, lick his balls, then put it in your mouth and suck it.

—Moment of terror: Angel knows that Louis is HIV Positive. He is still her boyfriend, but they only do safe sex. Somehow in her drugged state, she remembers to ask:

Give me a condom?

DONALD: For a blowjob?

ANGEL: Please?

Donald gives her a condom.

DONALD: OK, put on the condom and suck his cock. Do I have to guide you more or can you guys just go at it?

Ah, they're relaxed enough, he thinks to himself. And they are. They are perfect models. They please each other orally, both ways. He even eats her ass (with a make-shift dental dam). He fucks her, and while they are fucking she puts her finger in his ass. (Donald does have to instruct her to do that.) The boy comes and the girl comes or fakes coming at the same time. Donald wonders whether or not she fakes it. Most of the young girls don't know how to have an orgasm yet. Because none of the young boys know how to give one either.

Donald is really impressed with these two specimens. He is saddened to let them go. He never uses models twice.

10.
Public Service Announcement

3:05 A.M. Saturday, August 31.
Tacones.

In the Trip Out Room. Bae and Breezy are still lounging. Breezy has flower petals pasted underneath his eyes. He is wearing a teased brown wig and an ocean blue pattern polyester dress with jelly shoe pumps. He can't stop laughing at this commercial, which is programmed to play five times in a row, at the end of each playing, rewinding on screen to the beginning, then playing again. (René Suvuomo is an artist.)

(*On TV*)

VOICE OVER

This is a public service announcement reminding you not to leave your baby out in the sun . . . it could get eaten by dogs.

(*Cheesy music*)

Woman in red high heels, a red PVC bra, white bell bottoms, sunglasses, hair wrapped in a scarf, walks out and places her baby on a Disney's *Lion King* towel in the middle of a suburban yard.

WOMAN
Take a little nap, little Ashley!

She goes back into the house.

We see cars driving by.

We see rows of houses.

There is an overhead shot of the neighbourhood.

(*All houses match.*)

Back to the baby. CLOSEUP of its smiling, gurgling face. Suddenly a pack of vicious dogs charge across the lawn at the blanket, barking.

They fight over the baby, one finally getting a good grip on it, shaking it all about, eventually letting it go, when all the dogs pounce on it and tear it to pieces. Very gory. The dogs run away, a bit slower, down the street.

    CUT TO:

Mother coming back into the yard, going up to the blanket, seeing it smeared in blood, seeing something on the blanket, something left behind.

    CUT TO: CLOSEUP

The baby's hand, left behind by the dogs. The mother reaching into the frame, picking it up, shrieking.

CUT TO:

Mother clutching the hand to her chest, running back into the house, shrieking.

FADE TO BLACK:
VOICE OVER

Be careful. Be very careful.

Followed by crazy laugh, the unmistakable laugh of René Suvuomo.

Breezy is hysterical about the woman in PVC. "That looks like my mother . . . " he laughs over and over.

11.
Trevor Places the Ad

Thursday, August 15, 1996.
Toronto.

Time has passed. Months. He is ripped now. His body is toned. His skin is tanned. His tattoo is healed. He is the model of sexiness. So now what? he wonders. Does he start working as a "boy"? Or does he just live a life of beauty?

He puts in his new ad. This time he puts it in the classified. Not on the voice system:

> *HOT NEW BOY (12 pt. Bold Shadow Headline) 20 years old, 5' 11", 165 lb, solid muscular body, blue eyes, short dark hair, big uncut cock, shaved balls, smooth with hairy legs, tattoo, navel piercing. Creative, kind, intelligent. Hot man-to-man shower/ massage, mutual oral, cuddling, J/O, etc. YOU WON'T BE DISAPPOINTED. TREVOR 413-0536*

This is a new feeling for him. A feeling of excitement. The day that the paper comes out, he's still in the middle of painting his apartment. A bit nervous. The phone doesn't stop ringing. Some people phone literally every ten minutes. He finally answers some of them, to tell them that he isn't available until Tuesday. The paper comes out on Thursday. So he loses a lot of money over the weekend. But he has stuff to do until Tuesday. So he turns them down. He gets a taste of what it is going to be like talking to them on the phone about his cock and things like that. It is a very bizarre sense of power.

12.
A Date for Diva

3:07 A.M. Saturday, August 31.
Tacones.

The Back Room—lots of the kids hang out here. It's where they're allowed to smoke dope out in the open. The twenty-year-old hustler kids, a lot of drag queens, a lot of straight guys who don't know the drag queens are drag queens. Diva is here. Taking a break. There is a huge mix of people back here. Mostly smoking weed, or using the little cocaine room in the back—a converted closet with a shelf at nose level, some razor blades on those little chains like the pens at the bank, straws. All painted nice—purple and silver, mirrored walls, soft leather bench. There's a balcony for smoking crack too. (Everyone freaks if someone smokes it inside—smells too much like burning styrofoam.)

Steve is talking. He has likely smoked about three or four grams of weed in the past hour. "Guy, one day, you and me, we's gonna go out together—just us—for the night. Drop like three or four hits of acid, smoke a lot of weed, just get FUCKED, and go to the Buzz Club, maybe out on Queen West, back here, just have a good time, get away from things. What d'ya think?" He is talking to Diva. It doesn't make sense that he is relating like this to the bitter, nasty, beautiful faggot. Steve always kind of acts as straight as he can. Doesn't really talk to the gay guys. But now he's talking to Diva like this. Wanting to get to *know* him, it seems.

"Yeah," Diva says. "I'd be into that. That'd be wild. I usually hang out by myself, so it'd be kind of cool going with someone." Diva thinks to himself that it will be really cool. (Except for the weed. He hates weed.) Maybe he'll take Steve to the beach. Show him what it's like by the rocks. But he won't tell Steve that until later.

"Maybe next week," Steve says, walking away. Always in motion. Almost dancing around.

13.
Biff & the Boys

3:08 A.M. Saturday, August 31.
Tacones.

Steve, Biff and their friends are hanging out in the Back Room of Tacones, talking, playing pool.

Flex is seventeen years old, hangs out with Biff and his friends, tells them all that he's not a hustler, that he's not a fag, secretly has a sugar daddy that they all know about anyway, but he truly believes that no one knows a thing. Kind of a complicated kid. He's playing pool with Justice, a skinny punk rock sixteen-year-old kid who has an ad running in the paper:

Pierced punk slut tattooed Rim suck fuck lick. Dirty
eighteen-year-old skank. $80 Call 415-8755.

Louis and Angel are sitting at the side. Still a bit numb from Dennis Bell's needle. "You think you can get a trick tonight, babe?" Angel says. "I fucking want to get a room tonight. I want to take a shower."

"We'll see, Angel. I think that guy'll be here later."
"I WANT TO TAKE A SHOWER!"
"Don't fucking freak out, ok? The guy's been here every Friday night for the past month, ok? And he likes me. It'll be ok. You could fucking work the stroll for a change."
"I'm scared."
"Don't worry." Louis hugs Angel. They've been sitting pretty quiet in the Back Room ever since Mr. Bell tossed them out on the street. Their friends can tell something went down, but won't pry. Etiquette.

Steve punches Louis on the shoulder. "Hey guy, man, how's it goin'?"

LOUIS: "Not bad, man, not bad." This particular group of hustlers all believe that they're straight and pretty much deny that they turn tricks and talk a lot about robbing people and doing car thefts and shit—anything to avoid hustling.

Steve is part of this group. They hang out all day at the hustler bars, playing pool, every now and then discreetly leaving with a john, usually making the john leave two minutes before, meeting him two blocks away, walking twenty feet behind him, pretending not to be with him. All the boys in this gang do this all afternoon pretty much every day and none of them are admitting it to each other. Steve has spilled a bit to some people—talking about some of his johns and the shit he's done. He's done some pretty heavy scenes, actually—including a couple of shit and degradation ones.

A transsexual walks in. Biff and Steve stare at her.

BIFF: You like trannies?

STEVE: No, man.

BIFF: Yeah, man. Me neither.

STEVE: I mean, don't get me wrong, guy, I can be friends with 'em, you know?

BIFF: Oh yeah, man, I wasn't sayin' they's bad people. I live with one.

STEVE: Oh? You into that? That's ok, man. I won't be the one t'judge ya, y'know what I'm sayin'?

BIFF: No, no, no, man. She ain't my girlfriend, y'know? Just a pal. She lets me live with her.

STEVE: Oh. Good, man. I was gonna say—I mean, I won't judge ya if ya do like 'em, but man, I think they're kinda sick, if we're talkin' about bein' naked with 'em and shit.

BIFF: Yeah. You're right, man. Couldn't deal with the dick, you know what I'm sayin' bro'?

STEVE: Yeah, bro'. Give me five.

They high-five. Biff's been hustling now ever since he got out of jail. Doesn't like Nobia to support him any more. Doesn't want to risk any more B&Es because jail was a bit rough to him. Too much.

He does a couple more tricks and goes home and smokes weed with Nobia for hours while watching TV, and then begs her to fuck him up the ass—BEGS her. She does.

14.
Peony

3:08 A.M. Saturday, August 31.
Tacones.

Diva snorts another fingernail of coke and goes back up to work. He liked the attention from Steve. Momma is working the bar for him. She is a fairly hefty black woman who does a lot of the bussing and pretty much anything that needs to be done. "Y'alright, honey?" she asks Diva. "Yeah Momma, I think I got a date," he says. "Good work, baby, good work," she says.

The Nursery School Teacher staggers into the club. Six feet tall plus platform heels, hair swept up in a bun, sunglasses. She walks to the Back Room. Looking for a dealer she knows. Can't find him. Walks back out.

Peony flies into the club, bumping into Nursery School Teacher. "Out of my way, bitch!" she snaps loudly enough that everyone's head turns, and makes her entrance with her friends in tow. Two little boys. One just turned eighteen. The other nineteen. She's a twenty-nine-year old transsexual. She's beautiful. She's wild. She picked the name Peony when she started living as a woman because, "If you could pick your own birth name, wouldn't you make it glamorous and theatrical?"

She likes the young boys. "Grubby little boys," she calls them.

She goes up to Diva. "Did you hear about Elizabeth, girl?"

"No, what happened, girl?"

"She got fired from her sugar daddy's bar 'cause they caught her doing coke in the bathroom while she was working."

"It's not like she needed to work there."

"Oh no, I know, she just wanted a job. I mean, her sugar daddy would take over her bar for her while she left to do a client. She'd be on her cell phone behind the bar, stoned out of her mind, drunk out of her mind, breaking it down for guys on the phone what she was all about."

"She's wild," Diva says.

"Yeah, and so now that she's not working, she's going to go in and get her boobs done."

"She should do something about the hair extensions at the same time," Diva says.

"Oh my god, I know, they're brutal. She's such a tranni, for a real girl. Did you know, I worked the streets with her? She worked the tranni stroll instead of the real girl stroll. I never could figure it out, but she was always with us."

"You're reading, girl!" Diva snaps in his bitchy queeny way. He is other-worldly. Takes a drag on his ever burning Matinee

Extra Mild 100s Menthols "What can I get you, girl?"

Peony orders her drinks, buying for her little boyfriends too.

Last night she had come in with this hot teenaged jock guy. Diva had looked at her behind the boy's back and given her the thumbs up. "Totally whipped, girl," she said to Diva. "Would do *anything* I say."

"Really?"

"Hard. He's amazing. Needed some Kleenex, made him go get it for me."

"Good for you, girl. And make sure he gives you full service!"

"Uh huh!!! If she's gonna be with this trannie she's gotta be able to deal with the dick, you know what I'm sayin'!!!"

He gives her the drinks. She gestures to the boys to pick up the drinks, including hers, grabs her purse and flies off.

15.
Nobia & Biff

When Nobia met Biff, she asked him his name and he said "My name's Biff." Nobia smiled and winked at him and said "You're very cute, Biff." She knew it wasn't his name, but thought it was cute that he liked to pretend it was. He walked closer to her in a very pretend macho way and took her hand and kissed it. From that moment on they were a couple.

Biff moved in the next day. He didn't have a lot of money, except for when he did B&E's, which was maybe once every week or two. Nobia told him to stop doing that kind of stuff anyways, that she would pay for whatever he needs.

So to keep her happy, a lot of the time Biff sat at home and watched TV and she went out and worked on the stroll at night and met him at Tacones andbought him drinks and weed and occasionally acid or mushrooms. He wouldn't do cocaine. He didn't like it when she did cocaine, because he'd get horny later in the night and her dick wouldn't get hard if she did cocaine. He never told her that this was why he didn't want her doing it, because he was supposed to be straight, but she knew he wanted it well enough when he rolled over and begged her to put it in.

16.
Answering the Phone

1 P.M. Tuesday, August 20.
Toronto.

Trevor decides to start answering his phone. His ad has been running since Thursday and he is done what he needed to do over the weekend.

"Hello?"
"Is this Trevor?"
"Yes."
"I'm calling about your ad."
"Hi. How are you?"
"Fine, thanks. And you?"
"Fine. What would you like to know?"
"Your cock. Is it above average?"
"Yes. I would say so. It's not a . . . monster, but it's pretty big."
"In length, or in thickness."
"Both."

"What is your price?"

"$120 for up to an hour."

"Thank you. I'll call you when I've decided."

Trevor hangs up. He isn't shaking like he thought he would be. He kind of liked talking about his cock over the phone with a stranger. This is going to be work. The phone rings again.

"Hello?"

"Trevor, please."

"This is."

"Hi. You have an ad running?"

"Yes."

"I have some questions."

"What would you like to know?"

"How much is your rate . . . for cuddling . . . and I like to have my nipples played with. And I like to end it getting pissed on. In the shower, of course."

"$120 for up to an hour."

"Do you have transportation?"

"Oh. I only work from my apartment."

"Oh. You don't do outcalls."

"No. I'm sorry."

"OK. Thank you. Bye."

"Bye."

This is not totally easy. But he isn't depending on it for income right now. So it's fine. Entertainment. He's learning a new trade.

17.
Mr. Hammer

2:30 P.M. Friday, August 30
North York.

Is this the place? they wonder. Yes. They see the sign.

> SEND TURTLES TO MISSISSIPPI.
> RETURN THEM TO HEALTH & HAPPINESS
> IN THEIR NATURAL HABITAT.
> $5. FOR POSTAGE
> BE KIND TO ANIMALS

Mr. Hammer is in the back. He is the owner of the pet store. He has a big snapper on the workbench. He has worked the chisel into the shell and is hammering it. It's a tricky one. It doesn't seem to want to pop open. He gets frustrated and starts hammering at it madly, breaking through its tough underside in a few places. He doesn't care if the shell gets destroyed. He has enough ashtrays at his house. Finally the hammer goes right through with a sloshy noise. Turtle guts spill out and some fly through the air. He hears the bell ring at the counter. Wipes off his face a bit. Takes off his work apron. Goes out front.

"Hi. We found this turtle on the street . . . You tell him, Christopher."

The little boy looks up at Mr. Hammer, and in earnest says "I don't want Mr. Turtle to die, Mister. Can you send him back to Mississippi?"

"Of course I can, young man. I don't like to see turtles out of their natural habitat. Once they get into the suburbs, it's usually hard for them to find their way back to their ponds. Just leave him with me. And you know what? I won't charge you the $5.00 today. Save that for candy. For the good stuff." Mr. Hammer winks at the young boy.

"Thanks, Mister!"

Christopher's mother smiles at Mr. Hammer. She thinks it is so sweet that he has this service set up. Far too many parents are buying their kids pet turtles, and they eventually are outgrowing their tanks. She thinks it should be illegal to have pet turtles, but what can she do? Oh well . . .

"Thanks to you, Mr. Hammer, turtles can have justice too!" she proclaims.

"Say goodbye to the nice man, Christopher," she says.

"Goodbye, Mister!"

"Goodbye little boy," Mr. Hammer says, after handing

Christopher a yellow lollipop.

    The bell jingles, and they leave. He takes the box into the back room and tosses the turtle into a washtub, where it can wait its turn.

18.
An Ikea Moment

2 P.M. Saturday, August 31.
IKEA, Willowdale.

Sandra is shopping. She works during the week at a law office. She loves Ikea. It relaxes her. Her job really drains her. After work, she barely has enough energy to watch TV. She works from 6 A.M. until 7 P.M. She is shopping with her friend Stephen. He is not her boyfriend. Stephen is a celibate. Sandra doesn't have any romance in her life. She likes her job, though.

She looks at some papier mâché vegetables. Handpainted vases. Candles. A bed sitting in one of the displays with a mosquito netting over it. "The Malaria Bed," she titles it in her mind. It looks a bit creepy. Easy to visualize a bedridden old woman lying in it, hacking and coughing her way to her final moment.

Sandra sees kids everywhere. A little boy walks by, dragging an old bike handlebar on a yellow rope. "C'mon Randy," he calls to his imaginary pet dog. His brother follows, pulling a tuna can on a piece of twine. "C'mon Tuna." They are poor kids, whose parents have dumped them at Ikea for a couple of hours while they go out to dinner across the street at McDonald's.

A small girl knocks over an easel. She runs and hides her face in her mother's skirt. Her father sets the easel back up. All is well—it isn't broken.

There are miniature Ikea furniture sets for kids—teeny tiny sofas, teeny tiny coffee tables. Even a tiny office desk and chair set.

Sandra checks out the kitchen department. She doesn't really cook much. Ever, actually, but she thinks she should still keep a well-stocked fridge and cupboards in case anyone ever comes over. She picks up a frying pan. She likes it. She keeps it in her hand. Wanders through the glassware section. Sees some pretty glasses. Simple. Floral print. Nice. She makes a mental note to ask Stephen what he thinks of the glasses.

"MOMMMMMMEEEEEEEEEEE!!!!!!!!!!!!!!!!" a little boy screams and screams, running up and down the aisles from his sister, who is chasing him with a rubber snake. They pass Sandra and she smacks the little boy on the head with the frying pan, hard, three times, then drops the frying pan on the floor with a gasp of shock, horror, disgust, simultaneously throwing up. She falls down on the floor, landing in the vomit. She gets some of the little boy's skull fragments on her hand

and wipes her hand on her pants over and over, practically burning her hand from the friction, Stephen comes running. People are screaming. Gawking. The little boy's skull is cracked widely open. Someone calls for the police from their cell phone. The store security is sent for.

Stephen pushes through the crowd and leans over Sandra. "What happened?"

She shakes her head. Stunned. She doesn't know. She can't verbalize it. She had a loss of control. She has never done anything like this before. She has never even thought of doing something like this before. She lets herself be taken by security to the back room, where she will wait for the police to come cuff her.

19.
Oops!

3:12 A.M. Saturday, August 31.
Tacones.

Joan walks in. She's about seventy. She sits on a bar stool and drinks beer. She usually is carrying a cookbook or some other weird book. Tonight it is a book on drywalling. She pisses in her chair and periodically reaches into her purse and pulls out a loose piece of chicken and takes a bite. The chicken is unwrapped, in with her papers and money and dirty Kleenex. When Diva finally cuts her off and has someone help her to the door and up the stairs, the area where she was sitting looks like someone had a picnic. The bar stool is wet with pee, there are chicken bones, a banana peel and her TV Guide on the floor, along with some dirty Kleenex. Taxis won't stop to get her because she has pee all over her.

She is extremely rich. Her family owns one of the largest security companies in Canada. She lives in a condo on Bay Street.

Thirty-five years ago she was sitting in the living room of the beautiful Victorian house she shared with her husband Bruce, and her new baby Ashley. Bruce was reading the paper. Joan was holding the baby, who was crying. Joan had experienced a lot of pain during the birth, her first, and hadn't had a lot of energy since. She wished the baby would fall asleep, but knew that she would have to be selfless and learn to cuddle it and love it and nurture it. "Hello, Ashley," she cooed. "Honey, I'm going to take her up to bed, and I'm going to lie down myself for a nap. I'm still pretty drained."

"All right," said Bruce. "I'll be up in a couple of hours."

"Come on, Ashley," cooed Joan, picking the baby up. She carried the new baby in her arms, close to her chest, thinking about how serious this was, this new baby thing. Thinking about how no one had prepared her for the intensity of the situation. There were no lessons on how to be a good mom.

She mounted the steps. She walked slowly, trying not to jiggle the baby's head. She saw how fragile the neck was and imagined the head snapping off from her walking too unsteadily. She shuddered. She knows it's a grim thought, but she can't help but think these things. The baby is so small and so soft and . . .

At this point Joan tripped over her long nightgown and fell forward. In the desperate second before she landed on and crushed the baby, she tried desperately to get her balance, to put her arms far in front of her to protect her child, to turn sideways, to do *anything*, but she landed right on top of Ashley anyways and her little neck broke and she was still and Joan just lay there, uninjured. The baby had broken her fall, saving Joan from injury.

She lay there with the motionless child and in a fog noticed Bruce's anguished face looking into hers, faintly heard Bruce asking if she was all right, sort of felt the ambulance attendants putting her on the stretcher.

Bruce left her. A month after the accident, said "Things can't be the same; I'll always love you. But . . ."

Since then she has been in a state of shock. Very few senses are in full functional order.

Eventually, a taxi will always stop and help Joan home. Some good-natured driver, or maybe a driver who remembers her and knows that she always tips $5. no matter how short the drive home.

20.
Emaciated

5:30 P.M. Wednesday, August 28.
Toronto.

"Hello?"
"Hello. Trevor?"
"Yes."
"I'm calling about your ad."
"Yes. What would you like to know?"
"You have a good body?"
"Yes."
"Your cock is big?"
"Yes."
"You good-looking?"
"I like to think so."
"You are muscular?"
"Well, I'm getting pretty emaciated from the AIDS actually. I'm pretty skinny. I have to be honest."

Troy hangs up the phone. Laughs at his game.
Phone rings again.

21.
Isabel

3:20 A.M. Saturday, August 31.
Tacones.

3 Spanish queens come walking in. Hand in hand. Isabel Jurado, Nobia, and Denise Desire. They are a sight. Isabel is the most amazing to see at this hour of the morning. Tall, awkward body, very graceful walk. Very confident walk, for such a spectacle. Blonde, frazzled and teased wig, bad make-up—too much blush, blue eye shadow, bright lips. Big square manly features. Big shoulders. Not a lot of money for clothes. Sometimes wears polyester granny skirts and granny boots, with mesh, shawl-like tops. But so ugly she's beautiful. To some, the most beautiful of all the Latina queens.

She starts talking to Diva, who really likes her. Thinks she's flawless.

ISABEL: I am going back home in a month, back to Nicaragua. So you have to give me a kiss before I go.

DIVA: (affectionately) Girl . . . I'm not rough enough for you—you like big leather men . . . .

ISABEL: You are beautiful. You would spank me, no?

DIVA: I don't think I could spank you, girl . . . you're too nice to me. What is it like in Nicaragua? Can you dress up there?

Isabel gets visibly saddened. "No."

"Really? That's too bad . . . aren't there any underground places?"

"Well . . . yes . . . there is one . . . But very secret or we will get killed. It is in someone's basement and we would meet all together once in a while, about five or six of us, and drink beers and get dressed up. I am going back there though, so you must kiss me."

"You're coming back, aren't you?"

"I think so . . . I hope so . . . " Isabel seems sad, withdrawn, thinking about her country. She loves dressing up so much. She doesn't have the happiest life, but she tries so hard to be happy. She always comes out and tries to enjoy herself. "You are so sweet, darling," she says to Diva.

DIVA: Will you do a song for me?

ISABEL: What would you like me to do, darling . . .

DIVA: From that CD I got because I liked the way you did her songs . . . Isabel Pantoja.

Isabel's specialty is beautiful love ballads by the diva from Spain. Her long arms flail about spectacularly, her long press-on nails flitting everywhere, her lip-synching perfect with the tortured anguish prevalent in Isabel Pantoja ballads. Her drag performance is so powerful that when white people hear Isabel Pantoja's music by fluke, in restaurants, in record stores, or wherever someone's trying to be trendy by playing world music, they instantly think of Isabel, all dolled up, on stage.

ISABEL: What song would you like me to do?

DIVA: "Nada" . . . I think it's the seventh song on the CD. Do you know it?

ISABEL: Yes, darling . . . but you must give me a kiss.

Diva gives her a kiss—they slowly go towards each other's lips finally meeting in a very quick, but soft peck—her lipstick sticking to his chapped lips for a moment.

Isabel enjoys the moment, and then says, "I must go, darling . . . to the other room . . . but I will do the song for you. Next week. Goodbye."

22.
Piss Interests & Heroin

3:24 A.M. Saturday, August 31.
Tacones.

Ken is sitting at the bar. Forty-five years old, coke bottle glasses, fat. Self-proclaimed eccentric, high precision jewellery and watchmaker. Self-employed and wealthy, so can go on three week drinking binges whenever he wants. Talks pretty much about the same things, day after day. Every now and then starts talking a bit about sex. Always includes at least one reference to piss, almost with a subversive little shy giggle expression like, "I'm a naughty boy." Today he is talking to Warren, another old drunk guy.

> *Ken, to Warren:*
> "You hear about old Billy?"
> "No, what happened?"
> "He fell down the stairs."

"Again?"

"Yeah . . . " (chuckling) " . . . that's right. This time he had to go to the hospital."

"Really? Is he OK?"

"Oh yeah . . . You couldn't kill that one if you tried—he's fucking sixty-eight years old and he's been drinking since he was fifteen. He's not going anywhere . . . " (chuckling)

"He's gotta smarten up, y'know?"

Ken just laughs. Thinks old Billy's got the perfect life—up every day at 8:30 AM in time to work as a janitor at a bar where he gets paid twenty dollars in cash and twenty dollars in draft beer. Finishes cleaning at noon, sits at the bar staring into space all afternoon, starts drinking at four, drinks until he can barely walk, goes home at 2:30 AM, gets back up the next day and does the same thing. Almost seven days a week, with minor variations. Ken gets up.

"Gotta go drain the vein."

Ken walks into the bathroom, carrying his almost empty beer glass.

Dino and 'Julia' are talking near the door of the bathroom. 'Julia' is really Julio, but everyone calls him Julia. He talks like an elf. Or E.T. He has a weird voice. Long hair.

Ends up at the bathhouse at the end of every night after doing five or six hits of ecstasy, snorting a gram of coke, and drinking like a fish. He has been known to, on more than one occasion, go around regular bars at 2:30, right before the drinks are to be cleared, and pours all the last gulps and half bottles of beer into an empty draft glass and drinks it with a straw. "Backwash Cocktail."

Julia is very involved in the gay community, and the Spanish community. In the daytime he does all kinds of volunteer work for the AIDS Committee and others, and works as a social worker for a living. He doesn't really sleep, because he's up almost every night, all night, doing drugs and partying, but is also out volunteering and working every day. Shares a house with five friends, goes home maybe once a week.

He is a coke dealer as well, in a small-time sort of way. He was at another boozecan one day and someone accused him of selling "bad Spic coke" and actually pulled out his gun and said he'd blow him away if he didn't give him his money back.

In the background behind Dino and Julia, Ken emerges from the bathroom with a full glass of beer. It is a bit yellow though. And steaming. Dino and Julia don't notice. No one notices. He sits back at the bar and sips from his glass. Diva doesn't notice either. He has been starting to notice an odour around Ken, and has begun to think that Ken is pissing himself or not bathing.

Dino tells Julia "The other day, I'm here, right, and someone puts heroin into my drink when I went to the bathroom. I was fucked up for hours before I figured it out."

"Holy fuck."

"I haven't done that shit for over five years. I didn't even know what it was. I felt all fucked up and I couldn't figure it out. By the time I figured it out I was so pissed off that I couldn't enjoy it."

"That is fucking rude."

"I know. All's he had to do was offer me a line—I'd a sniffed it."

"Totally."

"I went up to my friend's cottage and fell into his lake. It was so fucking cold."

"Some people are fucked."

"I know."

23.
The Fight

4 A.M. Friday, April 19.
Little Italy, Toronto.

It's around 4 A.M. Winter is finally over, but the nights are still a bit cool. Nobia has done four dates, one, a tourist from South Africa who brought her out to the clubs and bought cocaine and drinks for her and gave her four hundred dollars and told her he loved her. She decides that she's worked long enough, takes a taxi home, climbs the steps on her gold stilettos and opens the door. She can feel the draft right away. Biff is watching TV. There is a hole in the living room window.

"What the fuck you do to the window?"

"Nothing."

"What the fuck you sitting there for? You sitting there all night with the fucking hole in the window? What's happening?"

"I forgot my key. So I broke the window."

"That window going to cost big money, you know? Who the fuck's going to pay for that, huh?"

"I'll do a job. Don't worry."

"When, huh?"

"Don't worry!"

"I don't understand you sitting there, boy. I fucking work all night and I have to pay the landlord now for this window. You could'a fucking come downtown and find me and I give you the key."

"Would you shut the fuck up!" Biff gets up and slams Nobia against the wall and punches her in the face a couple of times before she gets her bearings and slugs him—in the ear with her right, the nose with her left, right knee to the crotch, right hand grabbing his throat. "Don't you fucking hit me, don't you fucking hit me!!!" she screams and Biff is crying, feeling pathetic, like a little boy.

Nobia phones the cops and Biff sits on the floor crying and begging. "I'm so sorry, Nobia, I'm so sorry. I'll never hit you again," which doesn't work at changing her mind about the cops. She just sits on the couch and tries to cover up her blackened eye with makeup, wipes her bloody nose, occasionally glancing over at her crying baby, herself crying inside, but keeping an angry face on the outside. Pissed off.

Her makeup is perfect by the time the cops get there, and they can't figure out what to make of the situation. She's passable as a woman from afar, but not from police officers who want to see her ID and can hear her man voice. They can't figure out who the domestic assault charges should be against because he's sitting with a bloody face and she looks pretty good.

But Biff confesses, crying, and they take him to jail and the trial is set and he gets sentenced to three months.

She visits him a couple of times a week. She still loves him. Just thinks he should serve time for hitting her. He gets released after two months and moves back in with Nobia.

24.
The Perfect Fuck

3:28 A.M. Saturday, August 31.
Tacones.

In the back room, two beautiful boys are standing alone. These boys are stunning, model type boys. All decked out in their club kid wear. They have obviously been out dancing. They are shirtless and have perfect bodies. They are on ecstasy. They see each other and have a sort of chemical reaction— they are drawn to each other, take each other to the corner of the room, stare into each other's eyes. Stare into each other's eyes for a long time.

Silence, just staring.

One grabs the other's cock.

The other moves in and sucks the one's nipples. Licks him all over his chest. Grabs his cock. Goes down to suck it.

One stops him. "I'm HIV-positive," he says.

Other stops going to suck the cock. Stares at one in the eyes.

"Then kiss me," he says.

They kiss and kiss and kiss and melt and burn and drip. They grind and thrust and take each other's cocks out and jerk them while they continue to kiss, never letting go of each other's tongues. They cum onto the floor, feeling every pulse of cum come out of them. Their cum mixes together. They get napkins and clean it up. They both think what a perfect encounter it was.

25.
Ashley Sinks

10:30 P.M., Friday, August 30.
Lake Ontario, the Scarborough Bluffs.

Blaine and Carrie tie a rope around a sandbag and tie the rope to Ashley's waist and throw her in the water. The sandbag is barely heavier than Ashley, but as far as Blaine and Carrie can tell, she sinks. As the sandbag falls, they both heave a sigh of relief and just stare at each other. Their eyes lock and don't let go for about three minutes.

"Baby," says Blaine.

"Love you," says Carrie.

They drive the dinghy back up to shore. Grandpa wasn't up. He just yelled through the window that the keys were in the ignition, to take the boat. It is dark at this time, so no one sees them drop off the baby. They dock the boat and get out of there. First they smoke a rock. It is so peaceful, sitting in the little boat, hearing the water lapping against the rocks, smoking together.

They are very much in love at this point.

Ashley sinks for a while. Blaine and Carrie weren't Boy Scouts or Girl Guides when they were young, so their knots are not up to standard. As the sandbag falls, the rope slides off, leaving Ashley to sink on her own. The sandbag settles at the bottom. Ashley lands nearby. She will stay sunk for a while, but she will soon float to the surface.

26.
Bungee Jumping

10:30 P.M. Friday, August 30.
Canada's Wonderland, Vaughan, Ontario.

Peony, Stephanie, Pedro and Trevor all go bungee jumping. It is at an amusement park near Toronto. It's really more like simulated sky-diving. You are put into a harness with two other people, pulled from a hook on your back up to the top of a 150-foot high tower, and then dropped. The top of the cable holding you is attached to a 150-foot arch, parallel to the tower, and you swing. You can feel like Superman after the initial fear, and you can put your arms out in front of you.

Pedro and Trevor are put in the harness with a small boy who doesn't speak English. Stephanie and Peony are put into the other harness with a little girl who is by herself. Her whole family is watching. She must have gotten it into her head that she was going to do this thing, this frightening ride, with or without them. She proves herself to them.

The harnesses both go up at the same time. Trevor can hear Peony yelling "Tuesday!" all the way up. He starts screaming it back for fun. People down below probably are wondering what the fuck's going on. "Tuesday" is their code word for "Holy Shit" or various other things. Trevor and Pedro hold each other's arms, screaming all the way up. The little kid whimpers.

"Is he crying?" Trevor whispers to Pedro.

"Yes," Pedro laughs.

"Hold on to him, eh?" Trevor is scared for the boy. The workers gave them instructions really, really fast at the bottom: *Hold each other's arms at least until the end of the first drop, pull the rip cord at the top after the girl with the microphone counts to three. Don't pull it on the way up*—and Trevor is scared that the little boy who doesn't know English is petrified and has no clue what is about to happen. He can hear Peony screaming and yelping.

#1 and #2, on the count of three, release yourself—1, 2, 3!!!!!!

Trevor is the one who has to pull the cord on their side. Stephanie pulls it on the other side. They fall.

this feels so amazing i feel so good fuck crazy SUPERMAN i love this I LOVE THIS! gasp exhilaration holy fuck holy fuck TUESDAY TUESDAY TUESDAY Whoooh, shit! Motherfucker motherfucker motherfucker . . .

Their thoughts and words are incredible. (The little boy shrieks in Russian the whole way through.) They finally come to a stop and they meet on the other side of the fence and take a Polaroid. The little boy has run to his father and hugged him. The father smiles at Trevor and Pedro as they leave, saying "Thanks" for taking care of his boy. They are all fucked up from the experience. They all agree that it was one of the best days they've had in a long time. Talk about it for months to come.

Pedro and Trevor don't want to go home yet. The park is closing, this was their last ride. They get on the bus to go downtown.

"Want to go out to the beach with me?" Trevor asks Pedro.

"Sure." Trevor tells the girls he'll meet them later at Tacones.

Pedro and Trevor used to be involved. Fought a lot. Different ages, different goals. They still are involved though, somewhat. Once in a while. They feel close.

They take the streetcar to the beach. Go down by the rocks. Lie on the sand.

PEDRO: Hear you're becoming a hooker.

TREVOR: (*uncomfortable*) Oh yeah . . .

Trevor doesn't say anything for a bit, then:

"Surprise, surprise . . . I wonder who told you that?"

PEDRO: Yeah, it was him.

Trevor's ex always tells Pedro what's happening in Trevor's life. It pisses him off.

PEDRO: It's all right.

Trevor holds Pedro tight. "I miss seeing you so much. You're so amazing."

There's only two years age difference but Trevor feels older. Loves the little guy who there's been so much drama with. His little brother, sort of, in an incestuous kind of way. They have finally reached an understanding, it seems. They hug and kiss and hold each other. The ride fucked up their perceptions. In a good way. They are overwhelmed by life and experiences and just need to lie there in the sand, listening to the water for a while. They kiss each other and that is all. That is enough.

27.
BIASTO-GERONTO-PHILIA!

BIASTOPHILIA: (Biasto: rape or forced violation; Philia: attachment to) Refers to those who are only aroused when sexually assaulting an unwilling victim. The rapist loses interest if their victim submits. They need to see fear or tension in the partner.

GERONTOPHILIA (Alphamegamia—older man, Anililagnia—older women, Chronophilia—age difference, Graophilia—older male, Matronolagnia—older female). Some people have a sexual attraction for people who are significantly older than themselves. There are even rapists who only attack elderly women (anoraptus). Gerontophiles often prefer the compassion, intelligence, experience, and charm of people who have achieved their life goals and now live to enjoy and share life with others. Special dating clubs cater to the needs of gerontophiles, as do some bordellos. There is even a video called "Grandma does Dallas."

3 A.M. Saturday, August 31.
East York.

Jake pushes open the screen door of the nursing home. It is 4 A.M. The building is silent and dark, save for the occasional hacking cough of an old person. Jake has a hard-on already. It is pulsing, pushing against the fabric of his pants.

It almost hurts. He touches it and squeezes it. He knows which room to go to. He visited the nursing home earlier in the day, pretending to look for his grandmother. He saw which one he wanted then. Room 222. Esther McCracken. Seventy-six years old, almost four times his twenty years. He wants to feel her insides.

He slips into her room. She is sleeping. Her hearing isn't all that great. She is also mute. Which was part of Jake's attraction to her in the first place. He pulls off the blankets. Gets on top of her. She wakes up. Struggles, but is very weak. He holds his hands around her throat. She struggles, but more feebly. He pulls up her nightie, pulls down her cotton panties, pulls his cock out and shoves it into her. It's all dry and scratchy inside her. He shoves harder, not applying any lube. You like that, he says to her. She gasps. She can't scream. He takes his fingers from around her throat. She gasps more, taking in the air. He has gotten his cock all the way in her now, and he thrusts at her, gradually thrusting and twisting harder and harder. He stops. Lies dead weight on top of her. He wants to be with her for a while. This isn't just a get-his-rocks-off sort of situation.

He lies on her and then starts to make out with her, loving the resistance on her part, loving how she tries to turn her mouth away from him, keep her lips closed. But he's stronger and always gets his tongue into her mouth, sucking at her tongue and lips. She's so weak that she can barely resist him. As far as he can tell, she might even be liking it. It is like being trapped under a house.

He lies there for a while, kissing at her, poking at her sides, just lying there. He likes the feeling of her thin, bony, frail body under his. He starts to fuck her again. Her body is bouncing up and down on the bed. By now she is almost losing consciousness. Esther is actually wishing that she *would* lose consciousness. It would be better for her that way. Jake keeps fucking her, getting more into it, pulling her body up towards his. Eventually he flips her over onto her stomach and lies down on her, dead weight. This is fun, he thinks to himself. He doesn't want to leave, but knows he has to. So after teasing her anus with his cock for a bit, he flips her back over and fucks her again, this time until he comes inside her. He pulls out, kisses her again—even though at this point it is like kissing a dead person. He gets dressed and leaves.

They find her an hour later. She isn't dead. Just unconscious.

A week later, she dies. There are no findings in the autopsy to connect her death with the encounter. So Jake only committed rape, not murder.

28.
"SOOZI"

4:30 A.M. Saturday, August 31.
Tacones.

Jake has heard that there is an after-hours around here. He wants a beer. He is shaking. It felt so good with the woman back there. He can still feel her underneath him. He can still taste her tongue. He feels so amazing. Happy. He goes to the bar. Diva has stripped down to just his jock strap. Jake sort of stares, then orders a beer. Then a shot of Sambuca. Then two more. He picks up his beer and walks around. He sees Viviana, Denise Desire, Isabel, and Nobia. He can tell that they aren't real girls. Viviana comes running over to him "Ay, look at those cheekbones, we must put makeup on you darling, you'll be beautiful!"

Jake doesn't really follow what is happening next, but he ends up in the drag queen changing room, sitting on a stool, with Viviana applying a face to him. Isabel is crawling around at his feet, kissing his shoes, talking dirty to him. "I know you'd like to spank me darling, and I would like you to spank me too . . . " Jake is not too freaked out about this. He is still in shock from the events of the day. He has a hard-on again. And can't figure out why.

Isabel never misses a hard cock. She finds it, pulls it out and starts to suck it. She notices that there is a bit of blood on it, which kind of turns her on. She imagines that he is a straight high school boy who just fucked his girlfriend on the rag and that makes her almost cum in her pantyhose.

"*Mujere!!*" Viviana says, when Isabel keeps shaking Jake around, making the makeup smudge. "We have to get her ready for her big show!"

Jake's dick is throbbing. Isabel sucks madly. "*Mujere!!* Stop sucking the snake right now . . . . Get her her pantyhose!"

Isabel stops sucking and removes Jake's jeans, runners, white socks. She pauses to rub the socks all over her face, and the underwear too, sniffing the ass area especially. Jake is not a totally clean boy, thus producing the dirty ass smell that she loves. Flavour. Denise Desire has brought Jake three more Sambucas and another beer, which he accepts. Isabel pulls up his pantyhose, putting them overtop his erect cock. She sniffs and licks at it through the pantyhose. He likes the way the pantyhose feels against his cock.

Viviana is done with his face. She selects a dress for him. "Stand up, baby," she says. She pauses to do a line of coke. She offers to him. He declines. He lets her put him into the dress.

She gets a tape and puts it in the little ghetto-blaster. Presses 'play'. "OK, I teach you the words. It is duet. I perform it with you."

"I don't speak Spanish."

"Oh. Well . . . um . . . just move your lips 'round. Oh, look at her, she so beautiful!" Viviana squeezes Jake's cheeks, Denise and Isabel all come closer, adjusting his dress. "Wig!" says Denise. "Get her a wig!"

They position the wig. Jake is ready.

"What should we name her?"

"Soozi!" says Denise.

"HELLO SOOZI!" say Denise, Isabel, and Viviana all at once.

"Come with me Soozi." Viviana drags Soozi with her out into the bar. Jake is stunned. He has figured out what is happening. But nothing feels strange after what happened earlier. The Ultimate Experience. He actually thinks to himself, "Wow! I'm dressed as a woman about to be in a drag show, like what the fuck man," but doesn't care.

René Suvuomo has been informed that it is Showtime. "GOOD EVENING LADIES AND GENTLEMAN, Welcome to Tacones, Showtime!!! I would like to present to you, from Costa Rica, CON AMOR, Viviana!!!!! *with* Special Guest, SOOZI!!!"

The music of Azucar Morena starts to play. Jake and Viviana come out on stage. Jake sees the people, most of them staring at the stage, smiling and watching, so he starts to dance. He only knows how to dance hip-hop style, which is hard to do to a flamenco beat, but for the venue, it kind of works.

Soozi is a hit. She makes $45. in tips.

29.
Full Service

Steve is pretty dirty, underneath it all. Once he and his friend Jason had gone up to the office where Stephanie worked and asked if they could see her. (They had been introduced to her one night at the booze can. She had mentioned where she worked.) The receptionist looked at the grubby boys suspiciously and paged Stephanie. She came out and they all went to the donut store next door for a cigarette.

Everyone is nervous.

STEVE: You look hot today.

STEPHANIE: Thanks.

STEVE: Doesn't she, Jay?

JASON: (*not looking at her*) Yeah.

STEVE: Can I ask you something I wanted to talk to you about? Both Jason and I want to service you. I already know you like to have your pussy eaten.

STEPHANIE: You're joking, aren't you?

STEVE: No, I'm not.

STEPHANIE: Is this for real, Jason?

JASON: (*not looking at her*) Yeah.

STEVE: One of us would like to eat your pussy and the other could eat your ass.

There is an uncomfortable silence. Stephanie doesn't know what to say because in some ways the idea sounds appetizing. Jason kind of has B.O. right now, she notices, but she can always make him shower. After all, he wants to service her, so she can tell him what to do and he'll like it. But there's something about these boys that makes her a bit nervous, so she just remains silent. Doesn't want to invite them into her life. Can't quite figure out where to put the barriers, dividing her aboveground existence from her underground flirtations.

STEVE: Do you think I'm perverted?

STEPHANIE: No! Not at all . . . it's a natural desire.

STEVE: Oh. Well. Anyways, I didn't mean to disturb you at work. I just wanted to let you know that if you wanted it, we'd be happy to please.

STEPHANIE: OK.

STEVE: So just let us know, OK?

STEPHANIE: OK.

STEVE: Sorry for bugging you at work.

STEPHANIE: That's quite all right, hon, I wanted a cigarette break anyway.

Steve and Jason get up and leave the donut shop. Stephanie goes back to her office, torn. A bit moist.

30.
Scrap

11 P.M. Thursday, August 29.
Little Italy, Toronto.

Nobia comes home to find Biff masturbating to a gay porno. "What the fuck you think you're doing? Huh?"

He looks embarrassed and turns it off. "Nothing."

"You a faggot?"

"No."

"You want to be with mans?"

"No."

"It's OK, boy, if you a faggot you go away right now buy poodle whatever!"

"I'm not a faggot, Nobia," Biff shouts, jumping up. "I'm not a faggot!"

"OK then. You not a faggot. How you make you living?" (quick cock sucking hand gesture) "I know where you go all day!"

He is silent. Angry. Doesn't know what he can or can't say. Wants to punch her but remembers what happened last time.

"What do you want from me, man?" he finally says.

"I'm sorry," she says, calming down quickly. "I don't know. I just scared sometimes that you leave me for real man."

"You are perfect, baby. You're perfect. I wouldn't leave you for a dude."

"You still love me if I have operation?"

"Yes, baby. I promise."

"I go back to work and make some money and buy us some weed."

"All right, baby," he says, kissing her.

"You have any money for taxi?" she says.

He is ashamed, not able to support his girl. "I'm sorry. I don't."

She looks disappointed. He says, "Wait in the entranceway," and runs ahead of her downstairs. She locks up and follows. Watches from the front door as he looks at cars along the street. Sees him smash a window, get in, ten seconds later the engine running, he picks her up at the front door.

She gets in, leans over, kisses him.

"I didn't want you to have to walk, baby," he says as he drives her to the stroll. Lets her off.

"Love you baby," she says.

He drives away, drops the car off near home, walks back home. Watches more TV.

31.
Surreal Drug Art of René Suvuomo

6 A.M. Saturday, August 31.
The Trip Out Room.

Bae and Breezy are still chilling. They are leaning into each other. Their trip is slowly winding down, they feel a bit tired, but absolutely relaxed, giddy, waves of energy still passing over them.

On TV:

INT. CONFESSIONAL
Camera on empty confessional for a minute. RENÉ SUVUOMO *then walks into the room—actually bouncing and grinning and giggling. He is wearing a priest collar and a black robe and his own beret. His jerry curls are particularly large. He sits down on the chair.*

WOMAN'S VOICE

Bless me father for I have sinned.

RENÉ SUVUOMO

What have you done?

We see NANCY, *an upper middle-class woman in a beige skirt and a white blouse kneeling before the confessional window.*

NANCY

I have had impure thoughts. And I have done impure actions. And I have committed mortal sins.

RENÉ SUVUOMO

Oh Nancy, you slut, you been fucking your neighbour Ken again, haven't you? You been shooting the cats from behind the shed with your son's B-B gun.

CUT TO:

EXT. NANCY'S HOUSE, BACKYARD, DAY.

CLOSE UP: *Barrel of gun. Travel up to see* NANCY *holding it, wearing safety glasses.*

CUT TO:

CLOSE UP: *Big ceramic plate with steaming turkey and gravy on it. A beautiful Siamese cat walks into the yard and goes towards the plate.* NANCY *aims and fires.*

CUT TO:

CLOSE UP: NANCY's *face, safety glasses in place, ear plugs in place, smiling after the shot.*

CUT TO:

Beautiful Persian cat walks into the yard and goes towards the plate.

NANCY *aims and fires.*

CUT TO:

CLOSE UP: *The two dead cats, lying in front of the plate of turkey, still steaming. Another cat comes in.*

CUT TO:

Cat getting shot.

CUT TO:

Another cat getting shot.

CUT TO:

A pile of dead cats. NANCY *standing over them, smiling. A MAN wearing a judge's robe enters frame and silently hangs a sash over her—it reads "FIRST PLACE".*

CUT TO:

INT. CONFESSIONAL
RENÉ SUVUOMO *has stood up.*

RENÉ SUVUOMO

Yes, Nancy, you can go to hell for this. You can. You must repent. You must book yourself onto one of those Catholic tour bus trips and socialize with the members of the faith and go to casinos with them and drink with them and stay up all night in the hotels playing Monopoly with them and that will be your punishment.

NANCY

Oh father, not the bus trip. I can't bear the bus trip. Those people are fucking insane.

RENÉ SUVUOMO

Your choice . . . eternal hell, or the bus trip.

NANCY

I'll never shoot cats again!

CUT TO:
INT. CONFESSIONAL. DAY.
RENÉ SUVUOMO *is in his robe, doing a line of coke off the ledge in front of the confessional window. Someone kneels in front of the window.* RENÉ SUVUOMO *keeps snorting.*

MAN'S VOICE

Bless me father for I have sinned. I cheated on my wife of two years, Mary. By calling an . . . escort. And not just any escort. A SHE-MALE escort—that's a girl with a . . . you know . . . THING down there. And I wanted to suck it and I paid a hundred and twenty dollars . . .

RENÉ SUVUOMO

Is that you, Mario?

MARIO

Father René?

RENÉ SUVUOMO

Come around to the other side.

MARIO *comes around and sits on the floor against the wall. He is a stunning mid-20s stud.*

RENÉ SUVUOMO
You want some coke?

MARIO
You know I don't do that shit, father.

RENÉ SUVUOMO
How're you doing for cash?

MARIO
Not great. You know. Camaros drink a lot of gas.

RENÉ SUVUOMO
Yes. You wanna take your clothes off and I will buy you some gas.

RENÉ SUVUOMO *takes out 3 one-hundred-dollar bills and hands them to Mario. MARIO takes them and puts them in his pocket. Takes his clothes off.*

RENÉ SUVUOMO
Oh yes, Mario, that's a good boy. Oh yes . . .

RENÉ SUVUOMO *reaches under his robe and masturbates. He is very concealing of his masturbating—deep inside his robe. He is nearing orgasm. He grabs a couple of Kleenexes from a box nearby. Cums into the Kleenexes.*

RENÉ SUVUOMO
About that she-male escort thing Mario, go see her again. It'll make you feel good.

CLOSE UP: MARIO's *face*.

Bae and Breezy laugh hysterically.
"That was fucking rad, man. This guy's fucked."

32.
The Donut Shop

3:50 A.M. Saturday, August 31.
Parkdale.

Carrie goes up to the apartment to wait for the client. Leaves her cell phone with Blaine so that she can use the speed dial to call him in case of emergency. Blaine smokes another rock out back behind the store. Goes into the donut shop. Gets a coffee. Picks up a paper.

Starts to think about what happened with the baby. Can't help but think about it. "Why did I do it what does that mean about me ah fuck it had to happen though we couldn't take care of it I fucking hated my bastard father and I wouldn't want to have a kid hating me 'cause I wanted to party more. So I saved it. Abortion. Abortion is fine. There's nothing wrong with doing it after the kid's born. What's the difference." He is looking down at the floor. His shoelace is untied. He reaches down to tie it and he hears something land on the table. He jumps up. It is Ashley. She is normal looking, except for the blue colour of her skin. Then she explodes. It seems. Her head gets pulverized and her torso gets hacked up and her limbs separate and start to float in the air around him. Blaine's face contorts in horror. He stands up and tries to run away from the limbs. But they follow him. He tries to dodge his head through the legs, which keep closing together, blocking him. He is a human hockey net and the Ashley pucks keep moving around, growing and shrinking. People are staring.

"Sorry man . . . I smoke crack . . . I'm just freaking out a bit," he says, calming down.

The people staring at him save him from the baby parts. They distract him enough that the baby parts go away.

33.
Ashley Bobs

5:55 P.M. Saturday, August 31.
Lake Ontario, The Scarborough Bluffs.

Ashley is at the bottom of the lake. She didn't end up landing in a deep section. Only about fifteen feet. The rope is still tied around her waist and the loose end is floating above her, looking as if someone's tugging it. Her body is getting very close to floating. It bobs a bit with the slight motion of the water when a big boat goes by. She is wearing her pajama bottoms, her gold stud earrings. Her skin is very white.

34.
Trick with No Dick

3:50 A.M. Saturday, August 31.
Parkdale.

Carrie waits patiently for the man to phone her from the pay phone down the street. She is psyching herself up for it. She took a quick shower when she got in and feels a lot better. Had a small rock stashed in her purse and did a quick zap off it. She put on some makeup and some leather. The guy sounded like he'd be into that. She always tries to be prepared, to be as sexy as possible. No matter how high she is. She thinks she would lose her mind if she found herself losing her professionalism. The phone rings.

"Hello? Hi. You're at the pay phone. The one on the corner of Queen and Roncesvalles, right? OK. You walk a bit east to Triller Street. It's two blocks. You turn right and go to 32. It's a highrise. The buzzer is 304, OK? 304. That's the apartment number too. Just buzz and come up. OK, see you."

He's on his way. Probably excited. The buzzer rings a couple minutes later. Carrie puts out her cigarette and buzzes him in. She goes to the bathroom and gargles with mouthwash. There is a knock at the door. "Coming," she calls.

She opens the door. The man stands there. "Come in," she tells him. He obeys.

"You're beautiful," he says.

"Thanks," she says. She is glad that he thinks that. That gives her a boost. She figures it'll be an easy one. "Would you like anything to drink?" she offers.

He shakes his head. Just stands by the door.

"You can come in, you know," she says. He smiles. He is nervous. Very nervous. She is used to nervousness, but she notices that his is fairly severe.

She goes up to him and takes him by the arm and leads him to the couch. She strokes his cheek. "You're cute," she says. She examines his hands. They are small. She figures he has a small dick. "I bet you have a beautiful dick."

He laughs nervously.

She starts to move things along. "So, listen, what are you interested in getting into?" she asks him.

"I don't know," he says shyly.

She takes the aggressive approach then, realizing he's not going to talk. "Do you want me to fuck you up the ass with my eight-inch strap-on?"

He nods.

"Do you want me to humiliate you?"

He nods.

"Let's take care of the business part, and then you're going to get your ass into the bedroom and lie on your stomach and spread your legs," she snarls.

He nods and takes out the $200 and gives it to her. She counts it and nods at him.

"What are you waiting for?" she says, standing up. He gets up and starts to walk down the hall. "ON YOUR KNEES!" she barks. He gets on his knees.

"Lick the rug!"

He licks it.

She follows close behind and pushes him down with her heel in the hallway. He gasps and falls flat on his face. She holds him down with her one foot, while making him lick the other. He is excited. Moaning. She lets him loose.

"In the bedroom. Strip. Come on."

He strips with his back to her and lies down on his stomach on the bed.

"I didn't say you could lie on my bed!" she snaps.

He slides off the bed, avoiding letting her see his front side. He is on his knees, face on the bed.

"Let me see you wiggle that ass. Yeah . . . tell me what you want me to do to it."

"Fuck me," he says.

"PLEASE!" she says.

"Fuck me, please, ma'am," he says. She doesn't say anything.

"PLEASE!!! FUCK ME!!! HARD!!!"

She doesn't say anything. She watches him squirm, staying in his position. She likes to wait sometimes, make them figure out what they're supposed to say, rather than give them the lines.

"I need it. I really need it. Oh, I want your big strap-on inside me. I hope it's really big and really hard and I hope you fuck me really hard too."

She gets out her harness. Selects a dildo. Chooses the large realistic looking one. Dangles it in his face.

"Lick it!"

He does. Carrie puts it in the harness. Puts a condom on it. Lubes it up. Lubes his ass. Shoving her fingers inside, he squirms. She teases his anus. Shoves it in, slow at first. He gasps. It is large. When it is all the way in, she fucks him, hard, aggressive. Holds his head down. Fucks. After a bit, she tells him "Beat your meat! Come on, play with it while I fuck you!" She wants him to cum. Her high is going away. His body language goes a bit uncomfortable and he starts to cry. She isn't sure what's going on so she keeps fucking for a few strokes, and then realizes that he is crying. She stops.

"I've never done this before," he says, "I'm so nervous."

"It's OK. It is. We can talk if you want, eh? I'm here to do what you want. I thought this is what you wanted."

He keeps crying.

"Come on, hon, let's sit down and talk about what you want. You paid, eh, and I'm not a rip-off artist. I'm a professional. What do you want?"

Through his tears, "You were doing it right, really, I just . . . "
"What?"
"I don't have a penis. That's all."
Carrie is momentarily shocked. "Did you have an accident?"
"No. I'm . . . a . . . I was born a . . . woman . . . " he says.

She looks at him down there. He blocks it. She looks at his chest. There are scars under his pectorals. She can barely see it through the hair. She figures it out.

"Don't worry, hon, don't worry. No big deal, I understand. Really."

"I just feel weird . . . I didn't know who to go to . . . I don't really meet that many people who will get into what I want. I like girls . . . I'm saving for my operation . . . Oh I'm sorry to be talking to you about this . . . "

"Listen, if I can be blunt, you paid for the time, and you just shut up with all this apologizing, all right? You do what you want. Let's talk about what you want. You've still got some time left if you want to get into something."

"I don't know . . . I don't feel like sex any more."
"Do you want to talk?"
"Maybe."
"Go on. I'm a good listener. How long you been at this?"
"You know about this, don't you."
"Yeah . . . I know a lot of transsexuals. The business, you know?"

"I just can't meet anyone. I really can't. I try to meet other transsexuals—male-to-female transsexuals, but they're all fucked up . . . . They aren't into me anyways . . . and the girls I meet are freaked out by what's down there." He points to his vagina.

"You're really looking good. You really are." Carrie is starting to crave another hit and starting to lose interest. She regrets that a little bit, notes it as a change in her personality— she used to be a better listener but lately she can't last as long. "Can you excuse me for a second?" she says.

The man nods. Carrie goes to the bathroom, grabbing her purse on the way. There is some more cocaine in there. That should tide her over until the good stuff. She snorts a couple of lines and goes back to the bedroom. The man has dressed. "I feel really stupid. I really do. I'm so sorry for wasting your time."

"It's all right, hon, it is," says Carrie, feeling a lot better and a bit clearer. "You'll do all right . . . . I admire people like you 'cause you're working for something you like, you're doin' your own shit, you're survivin' and that's good. You look really good. I would never know."

The man smiles shyly. "Thank you. Thank you. It was nice meeting you."

"Likewise," says Carrie. The man leaves, head hanging low.

Alone, Carrie shakes her head. People are weird, she thinks. She really did like the guy, though. She felt bad for him. She phones Blaine at the donut shop. "Hey. He's gone."

"Already?"

"Yeah. Weird story. Tell you later. Meet you downstairs, OK?"

"Yeah."

"Actually, I'll meet you behind the donut shop. Get the pipe ready. I'm crashing hard. And don't let those fucking free-loaders near you. This is our money, they can fuck off."

"OK. See you in a minute."

She throws on some clothes, does another line of coke, and runs down the stairs to meet Blaine. She feels pretty good.

35.
Ashley Rises

9 A.M. Monday, September 2.
Lake Ontario, The Scarborough Bluffs.

Ashley's body slowly rises to the surface. Her skin is very white. The sun has started to heat up. The sky is perfect. Sailboats have started to clog the area. Kids are running around the sand, screaming. Tourists are walking the boardwalk. It is Labour Day. A motorboat cruises by, clipping Ashley's leg, not feeling the impact. She swirls and spins for a bit and then floats calmly once again.

36.
Crowd Thins Out

6:50 A.M. Saturday, August 31.
Tacones.

The crowd has thinned. Isabel is sitting on a chair with her legs spread wide apart, making fishy lips to anyone that walks by. Her pantyhose are badly ripped. Her wig is crooked. She keeps spreading her legs wider and wider. Opening them. Closing them. Hanging them over the side of her chair. Pouting. Putting on a show for anyone who is watching.

Trevor is the only one watching. He has smoked a lot of weed. He's just started escorting in the past few weeks. No one really knows this. Doesn't hang out in the clubs a lot. Comes out once in a while and visits his freak counterparts. Has his bonding moments. He loves them. Doesn't think they are freaks. He really likes Isabel. She has done drag shows at all of the bars he's worked at. She is the underdog. He is watching her. She doesn't see him.

Last call is announced at the bar. René Suvuomo has decided to close the main bar at 7:00 today. People will probably stay in the V.I.P room until about 10:00 or 11:00. Isabel jumps up and gets her final beer. Sits back down.

Those left in the bar are pretty much frozen, numbed images of people. Sitting next to each other talking about almost nothing—two minute pauses between each sentence. A couple of people passed out on the floor—earlier in the night if they were like that they'd be kicked out, but at this hour no one cares any more.

Diva is counting his tips. Momma is counting the cash. René is in the V.I.P room still carrying on with some of the cokeheads. Laughing, telling stories about Colombia, joking about family. René's mother is doing up the last loads of dishes, walking around with a bus pan, picking up cans and cups and drug baggies. Finds a couple of hypo needles in the bathroom, puts them in the tray as well.

Isabel keeps lifting her skirt, aerobically. As if she's flashing someone right in front of her. But there is no one there.

Jim staggers in. Trevor turns his head to hide his face. Jim is the worst. Trevor works part time at a bar, and kicked him out earlier this week. Jim drinks and drinks and drinks. He is young and was probably attractive a year ago. Apparently used to be able to be sober enough to hustle a bit. Now he can just look sober long enough to order a drink. Then he passes out. Trevor's heard stories about Jim being violent, so he's a bit nervous about Jim seeing him. Doesn't want his ass kicked over something so stupid.

Denise Desire comes up to Trevor.

"Trevor. Darling. Are you coming?"

"Where?"

"Come on!"

"What?"

Trevor is confused. Denise is standing by the door, waving for Trevor to follow her. He goes up to her.

"I'm going home."

"No. Come with me. Trevor. Come with us."

"Where?"

"Back to my place for drinks. Come on."

Trevor declines and tries to go back to his seat. It is getting a bit intense.

"Don't disappoint me, Trevor. You're disappointing me!"

Trevor almost feels guilty. Kind of spontaneous. Doesn't really want to go back to her place, but is fascinated.

Isabel is spreading her legs. Open and closed. Open and closed. "Trevor . . ." she calls. He goes over. "Yes, darling?" "Trevor . . . I want to suck on cock tonight . . . I really really really do . . ."

"I'm sure you'll find some . . ." Trevor doesn't know what else to say. She is a mess, posing and spreading and standing up and walking like a hooker and sitting back down and lifting her skirt and kissing at the air. He knows she wants to suck his cock. He knows Denise Desire feels the same way. He lights another joint and smokes it. Passes it to Denise and Isabel.

Jim orders a beer and walks by Isabel. "Darling!!!!!" she

calls out at him. He comes over. Trevor doesn't hear what she says, but hears Jim respond loudly, "Sure, I'm horny. I'd have sex with just about anyone right now. Just about anyone."

Isabel is standing up. Getting ready to go. Denise is still trying to get Trevor to follow her. They are both taking Jim back with them, it seems. Trevor likes Isabel, feels protective, goes up to her and takes her aside "Lookit, I know you want cock, but don't touch him . . . he's really dangerous."

He sees the look of sadness on Isabel's face. She doesn't want to hear this. This is the perfect person to go home with, someone who says out loud "I'd have sex with just about anyone right now" and Trevor realizes that he can't stop her. Can't protect her. He almost wants to offer himself so that she'll stay away from Jim.

"Just be careful. Please. Be careful with him. He's bad."

"Bad?" she says. She is like a child at this point.

"Yes. Bad."

"All right darling . . . I be careful . . . " She kisses him on both cheeks, Spanish style, and goes back to Jim and grabs him by the arm and takes him out.

Denise stands by the door, calling "Trevor! Trevor! Come with us." He thinks, "What the fuck," and goes to the door and leaves with Denise, Isabel and Jim.

37.
The Car

7 A.M. Saturday, August 31.
Toronto.

Trevor lets Jim and Isabel into the back seat. Jim sees Trevor for the first time and realizes who he is. "You!" he says, but that's about it. He doesn't threaten him.

Denise has a 1996 Camaro. "What do you do for a living?" Trevor asks her. "I work for factory. Fifteen years, since I came to Canada same job." She is also a street hooker, but she doesn't tell Trevor that. He knows, anyway.

Isabel already is sprawled across Jim's lap getting her bare ass slapped. He feels her cock getting hard on his legs. "You have a dick," he observes. This is the first point in time that he realizes she's a man. He doesn't care. She fits into his parameters of who he'd have sex with right now—Anyone. He keeps slapping. She really likes this.

Denise drives the car flawlessly, considering how much

she's had to drink and snort and smoke. The early morning traffic is starting. People going to work, going to the cottage, going to the market. Denise weaves in and out of them, Isabel in the back with her legs up in the air. Isabel is getting very involved in this now, talking very dirty and very loud.

"Darling I want you to BEAT me when we get home, slap me on my face, on my ass, on my chest. Make me suck your cock. Make me lick your ass."

Denise asks Trevor, "Do you like work at the bars?"

"It's all right."

She is a bit surprised that he is coming over.

Isabel is sucking Jim's cock. He comes in her mouth, noisily, and she swallows it all. "*Mujere!* Don't mess up the seats!" Denise calls back. Denise looks at Trevor. She thinks he is beautiful. He can tell this, and is a bit uncomfortable now. He is in the wrong place at the wrong time. He asks to be let off at the subway. Denise objects but finally complies. He leaves. Goes home.

38.
Isabel Weeps

7:20 A.M. Saturday, August 31.
Little Italy, Toronto.

Denise pulls up to her house. It is in Little Italy. It is a two-storey house. She bought it when she first moved to Canada with money she had brought with her. The neighbours are family oriented, foreign. They sometimes see her drive in at strange times of the morning, dressed up, but they don't make the connection that Denise Desire is really the Mario Pomella that they know. She's sucked most of the neighbourhood boys' cocks, dressed as Denise. So has Isabel. Or she's watched.

Denise lets Isabel and Jim out of the car. She sees that some cum has spilled on the seat. "You bitch, you got cum on my seat!"

Isabel howls with laughter and licks the seat clean. Jim thinks this is pretty funny. Denise shakes her head. She is suddenly ready to go to bed. Kind of grumpy. Isabel is still looking forward to spending some time with her man.

"Come on darling . . ." she says. He follows her. The house is a bit messy, but comfortable. Lots of furniture. Lots of places to socialize. It looks like there was a party there earlier.

Isabel takes Jim to her room. In the basement. She has a leather shelf set up. She has been pouring all of her money into this room. Full dungeon set up. People actually pay good money to come over and be degraded by her. But what pleases her is getting her ass fucked. And being spanked. By almost anyone. Because when she is out on her own terms looking for men, she almost never gets what she wants. It only happens once in every couple months that anyone comes with her and makes her happy. She has men of all shapes and sizes, some beautiful, in her basement all the time, tied up while she whips them, but she never gets anything for herself. She throws herself at Jim's feet and begs him to kick her. To get rough with her.

He looks at the leather bed. Looks at the room. Sees another room off to the side, with a normal bed on it. Says, "That the bedroom?"

She says, "Yes."

He goes into the room and lies down on the bed and passes out.

Isabel cries herself to sleep on the floor.

39.
Speed

3 P.M. Monday, September 2. Labour Day.
Lake Ontario, The Scarborough Bluffs.

"You want a martini, baby?" asks Wolfe. "Sure," says Stephanie. "Vodka, no vermouth, a lemon, please."

They are cruising around the Bluffs in his cigarette boat. One of his boys is driving the boat. Stephanie and Wolfe are lounging around, drinking martinis.

"It's fabulous outside, eh?" Wolfe says.

"It is, isn't it?" she agrees.

Once she said to her friend, about Wolfe, "He's really sweet, for a pimp," and they laughed hysterically at that statement. Wolfe owns Stud Farm Escorts, the biggest escort service for men in Toronto. He drives a green Jaguar, owns two boats, a house in Rosedale. He has all kinds of weird connections with prostitution. Once he offered Stephanie $1000 to go on a date with the guy from *Lifestyles of the Rich and Famous*, who likes to have tall beautiful women with him in public, then likes them to degrade him back at the hotel. Wolfe doesn't know that many tall, beautiful women, and figured Stephanie might be able to pull it off. So he went up to her and proposed the idea at her office. She's the person who takes care of the Stud Farm Escorts ads at the paper. She declined the offer. ("I'm a professional . . . ") So he asked her on a date, instead. This is the date.

She likes feeling glamorous. Riding in a boat driven by one of the Stud Farm boys. He had even offered to provide a boy for her. Usually they didn't do women, he had said, but for him . . . But she had declined. If her pussy is going to be licked, she wants Wolfe to do it. He is downright dreamy, she thinks. She wants him to service her. It is true, what Steve and Jason said, that she loves getting her pussy licked. She doesn't know that he doesn't service women. That in bed he is actually pretty boring. For some people it's hard to be interesting in bed for fun when it's your job.

The boat goes over a bump and there is a horrible noise in the propellers that sounds like something is being ground up. Stephanie looks over the back, martini glass in hand. The driver stops the boat and reverses the propellers to spit out whatever has gotten caught in them. Wolfe looks over the back, martini glass in hand. "Hmm. I don't see anything. Try it again," he calls up to the boy. The boy turns the propellers back on, and they spin smoothly again.

"Maybe we hit a big fish," Stephanie giggles. Wolfe smiles.

Tacones (High Heels)

"Want to see how fast this baby can go?" he asks.

"I'm ready!" she says. Stephanie is always ready for adventure.

"Come sit next to me. It's best up there."

Wolfe takes the driver's seat. Stephanie sits next to him. The driver goes underneath, into the cabin. Does some coke. Turns on the TV. Puts in a video.

Wolfe revs up the engine. "Hang on tight, baby," he says, and aims the boat straight out away from the Bluffs. The wake from the sudden increase in speed mixes and separates little Ashley's limbs and mushed up parts.

Stephanie stands up and puts her face over the windshield. She feels like a dog hanging its head out of a car on the highway. It is an unbelievable feeling. The boat hits 100 MPH. Her hair is flying. She starts to shriek. Shrieks of enjoyment. Wolfe is intensely focused on driving. He looks over at her. Sees her expression. Knows that she understands how he feels about his boat. About speed. Takes an instant liking to her. He didn't know, before. She is pretty, but that doesn't mean that he can relate to her. But now he thinks he can. They speed onwards.

In the cabin, the boy starts to masturbate. (He is bored.)

ABOUT THE AUTHOR:

TODD KLINCK is 22 and has been studying and living in Toronto subcultures for several years. He has been a university student, an after-hours security guard, a bartender, a porn model and has done production work in the film, television and animation industries. He is currently working on a video project, *Nursery School Teacher Tries Crack*, a screenplay adaptaion of *Tacones*, as well as a second novel, *Us Whores*.

PHOTO: TONY LONG

The Annual International 3-Day Novel Writing Contest
Every Labour Day Weekend

QUITE POSSIBLY THE WORLD'S MOST NOTORIOUS LITERARY MARATHON, THE CONTEST NOW ATTRACTS DARING AND ADVENTUROUS WRITERS WORLDWIDE.

How It Works:

Entrants must register by the Friday prior to the long weekend (postmarked). Writing begins no sooner than 12:01 a.m., Saturday, (basically, Friday night), and must stop at or before 12 midnight of the holiday Monday. Novels may be written in any location (yes, the honour system still exists!). First prize is an offer of publication and world-wide fame. Entry fee: $25.

Some further guidelines: 1. Outlines are permitted prior to the contest; however, the actual writing must take place during the Labour Day Weekend. 2. Collaborations are permitted, but no more than two per novel. 3. There are no limits as to the novel's length, but entries average 100 typewritten pages, double-spaced.

For a complete copy of the rules, send a SASE or fax request to the address below.

Published copies of past 3-Day Novel Contest winners may be ordered from Anvil Press: #204-A 175 East Broadway, Vancouver, B.C. V5T 1W2 CANADA Tel: (604) 876-8710, Fax: (604) 879-2667, E-MAIL: subter@pinc.com

Please include $2. per book for shipping & handling.

Previous 3-Day Novel Contest Winners

- **BODY SPEAKING WORDS** / Loree Harrell
  1995 winner 1-895636-09-4; $10.95
- **STOLEN VOICES/VACANT ROOMS** / Steve Lundin & Mitch Parry
  1993 double winner: 1-895636-06-X; $9.00
- **A CIRCLE OF BIRDS** / Hayden Trenholm
  1992 winner: 1-895636-03-5; $7.95
- **O FATHER: A Murder Mystery** / Bill Dodds
  1990 winner: 0-88978-229-6; $7.95
- **WASTEFALL** / Stephen E. Miller
  1989 winner: 0-88978-220-2; $7.95
- **PAWN TO QUEEN: A Chris Prior Mystery** / Pat Dobie
  1988 winner: 0-88978-209-1; $6.95
- **STARTING SMALL** / James Dunn
  1987 winner: 0-88978-195-8; $6.95
- **HARDWIRED ANGEL** / Candas Jane Dorsey & Nora Abercrombie
  1986 winner: 0-88978-190-7; $5.95
- **MOMENTUM** / Marc Diamond
  1985 winner: 0-88978-179-6; $5.95
- **NOTHING SO NATURAL** / Jim Curry
  1984 winner: 0-88978-167-2; $5.95
- **THIS GUEST OF SUMMER** / Jeff Doran
  1983 winner: 0-88978-151-6; $5.95
- **STILL** / b.p. nichol
  1982 winner: 0-88978-146-x; $4.95
- **ACCORDION LESSONS** / Ray Serwylo
  1981 winner: 088978-122-2; $4.95
- **DOCTOR TIN** / Tom Walmsley
  1979 winner (out of print)